Adam Gopnik

THE STEPS
ACROSS
THE WATER

illustrated by Bruce McCall

Disney • Hyperion Books

New York

First Edition
1 3 5 7 9 10 8 6 4 2
V381-8386-5-10213

Printed in the United States of America
Library of Congress Cataloging-in-Publication Data on file.
ISBN 978-1-4231-1213-6
Design by Michelle Gengaro-Kokmen
Reinforced binding

Visit www.hyperionbooksforchildren.com

For Olivia, citizen of every city she imagines,
rose and lily of our lives

Obviously

Chapter One

ACROSS THE BRIDGE

If Rose had been looking the other way when Oliver was talking to their father, she might never have seen the crystal staircase suddenly arch over the Central Park lake, and the two small figures looking carefully at Rose before skipping over the steps.

"Look!" she called out.

But by the time anyone did, the steps had already begun to recede, noiselessly, into the lake, shimmering for a moment, like an image going out of focus on a television set.

It wasn't exactly a lake—just a pond, really—but it was right in the middle of Manhattan, the densest and most crowded borough in the city of New York.

Rose was trailing behind her brother, Oliver, and their father as they tossed a football back and forth on the great oval lawn.

It was a perfect fall Sunday in the park, high October, and a cool breeze cut through the sunny afternoon. Leaves and litter skimmed across the lawn. Gusts of wind caught Rose's dress and teased it slightly upward, clutching it to her around the knees as she tramped through the leaves.

The sun cast long, golden, slanting shadows along the edge of the grass. Gone were the shouting summer crowds of softball players and barefoot Frisbee catchers. Only old couples sitting on park benches were left, and harried-looking students turning the pages of their books, which the wind tipped over. A few dogs pulled at their leashes on the walk that encircled the lawn, but their owners didn't let them wander onto the grass.

Rose sighed. She wanted a dog so badly. But she could never have one, because her mother was allergic to dog dander. Even when they went to a pet store, her mom wept and sneezed.

Oliver and her dad threw passes back and forth in the long shadows, and encouraged each other with congratulations and shouts. A single pink helium balloon from a child's birthday party floated away in the sky overhead.

All around the park the great towers of Manhattan loomed, crowding around as though they were giants on tiptoe, struggling to look down at the people at play. Looking east, Rose could even see the twelve stories of the apartment building where she lived. Looking south, she could see Belvedere Castle and the mysterious hills and paths of the Ramble that lay behind.

And that was when she saw it—a glass staircase sweeping up as suddenly as a rainbow, arcing across the lake at the end of the lawn. On the steps, two tiny figures in long overcoats, with one wreath of smoke around their heads, raced up and across the steps, taking quick, frightened looks backward.

"Look—there are steps across the water!" Rose exclaimed, pointing toward the lake.

Oliver and their father stopped playing catch.

"Where?" asked Oliver.

"Right there! Look! Right there!"

But the steps were gone by the time they turned around.

"That's very nice, sweetie," her dad said. Rose could tell by his tone of voice that he didn't believe her.

"Dad!" she said. "I really saw something—glass steps going out across the water. And two children running across them."

"*Rose*. You're just looking for attention," Oliver said.

"I am not. I saw them. They were real."

"*Rose*," Oliver said.

"Don't 'Rose' me," Rose said.

"Well then, stop making things up."

"I didn't!" Her bottom lip began to quiver.

"Oh, toughen up a bit, kiddo," Oliver said.

Rose turned and started running away back down the path toward the park gate. They always treated her as if she was . . . little. Even a baby. Oliver teased her about being young, and small, and though she knew he didn't really mean it in a cruel way, it was still incredibly annoying.

"Oliver!" warned their Dad, running after her. He tried to scoop her up. She resisted.

"Baby, Ollie didn't mean . . ."

She looked out longingly at the people who were walking their dogs at the edge of the lawn. There were big dogs and little dogs, snarly dogs and yappy dogs, ugly dogs with long snouts and sharp ears, and beautiful dogs with soft ears and fluffy coats. Every dog had an owner at the end of its leash. It was as if there was a magical connection between them, Rose thought: each person would never be lonely as long as they had their dog, and each dog knew that he could never be lonely as long as he had his owner. . . . If she had a dog, at least *he* would believe her about the steps.

Now Oliver was there, too. He put his arm around her and drew her close and kissed her still plump and blooming cheek.

"Hey, I'm sorry, Miss Tubs," he said. He was really very

fond of his little sister. Rose pulled away a little bit. But only a little.

Suddenly, a loud flutter of wings rose from the other end of the Great Lawn. They all turned. A flock of gray pigeons, hundreds of them, was flying from the trees on the east side of the Great Lawn, toward the West Side.

"What's making them do that?" their father asked.

"There must be something chasing them!" Oliver answered. Rose couldn't help but look up, too. She saw a single red-tailed hawk swooping down toward the terrified pigeons.

"It's the hawk! It's Pale Male!" Oliver said.

Rose remembered having read once about Pale Male, the famous hawk in New York City that lived high up on the balcony of an apartment building on expensive Fifth Avenue. For a while, the rich people who lived there tried to get rid of him: some people said it was because he was a nuisance, and others because he wasn't paying any rent. But lots of children and other sane people signed a petition to let him stay in his nest, and he did. This was good for everyone but the pigeons in Central Park.

Oliver laughed. "Go, Pale Male!" he shouted.

The pigeons seemed to make it safely into the leaves. The hawk hovered above the lawn, circling it, and then suddenly zoomed right out of the sky toward the western trees. The terrified pigeons, with the same clatter and coo, all flew in a dark gray cloud back across the lawn.

"Go, pigeons!" Rose whispered to herself. Her heart held tight as she watched them all make it safely across the way.

"What happens to the baby pigeons? I've always wondered," Rose asked their father, after she was sure the gray city birds were hidden in the trees.

"*Rose*, don't you know that's the oldest question in the book?" Oliver said, laughing. "The answer is . . ."

Their father's cell phone sang out, and he picked it up. He seemed to spend half his life on his cell phone.

"Just a second, baby," he said. "I'll get right off."

"Hey, Rosie," Oliver said suddenly. "Look what I found." And he pointed to a small dead mouse.

Rose made a face.

"No, it's good for the hawk!" Oliver said gently. "Hawks are always hungry. And this one doesn't have a mother to find him delicious tidbits. I read all about it. He's a motherless hawk."

"I don't exactly feel sorry for him," Rose said. "I mean, it's sad when anyone doesn't have a mother. But he's making a lot of motherless pigeons."

Oliver ignored her. "He's hungry. We have to take care of him. Look—we just have to put it on something bright that he can see from high above so that he'll notice the scrumptious smelly dead mouse carcass."

Rose knew that he was trying to make her shudder, so she ignored him.

"I know!" he said. "My sock!" And without another word he untied one of his sneakers, pulled off his bright red athletic sock, and carefully laid the dead mouse upon it.

"Mom will be furious at you for using your sock as a mouse plate," Rose whispered.

"I'll tell her you took it to make a puppet with," he said. She must've looked worried, because he added, "No, not really. I'll think of something. But how can Pale Male miss *that*?" he said, pointing at the sock. "A delicious mouse on a red platter. Mmmmm!"

Rose still felt queasy, and she didn't want to look at the dead mouse, of course; but she was impressed, as she often was, by her brother's practical mind. For, only moments later, Pale Male the hawk did come swooping down, grabbed the mouse in his ferocious talons, and then flew away again, as Oliver jumped with pleasure. She did, too, though she looked as she jumped, to see if the steps across the water had reappeared.

"I *did* see something, Oliver," she hissed a few minutes

later, as they turned down a crowded street, the empty park and their lagging father behind them.

"Hey, Rosie, if you say you saw it, you saw it," he said calmly. But Rose knew that he meant just the opposite.

"I did see it," she said. "It was the weirdest thing I've ever seen in U Nork!" Her heart fell in her chest as she said it. Now he would really tease her.

She had meant to say "New York." But Rose had a mild speech impediment, and often when she was excited, she switched around the first sounds of words. When she meant to say "good news," it would come out as "nood gews." And sometimes when she was trying to say "nice time," it would come out as "tice nime." And sometimes when she told people where she came from, instead of saying "New York," she would say "U Nork." This kind of thing seems very cute to older people when you are small, but becomes very annoying as you grow up. Her parents had taken her to the First Expert, who gave her exercises like saying sentences very slowly—but it would still happen. When the Second Expert's exercises didn't work either, he had taken her parents aside and whispered something about "speech impediments" and "traces of early trauma."

That's when they told the Expert that Rose was adopted. Her parents, who had wanted a little sister for Oliver, had gone to Russia and found Rose in an orphanage. They brought her home with them when she was barely two. Rose could just recall the orphanage in Russia—a big white room with a cold breeze blowing through it, and many warm hands picking her up and putting her down, and another little boy . . . but Rose couldn't remember anything more.

For the rest of the walk home from the park, Rose thought about being adopted. Something about the wind in the park, and the teasing, and the steps across the water made her feel the longing that came to her at times to know who her real parents were, and what strange things might be found outside her little world. She loved Oliver and her parents . . . but Oliver was always busy with his own friends, and her parents, well, they were parents.

Rose was lonely, and she wished she wasn't.

Even at school, though she tried hard to be a good friend, she often had the feeling that no one at school really liked her. Except maybe little Ethan, and he was so moist-eyed and solemn that it was almost the same as not having a friend. Actually, little Ethan was kind of like a puppy, she thought, and the thought made her smile in a sad kind of way.

She didn't say another word on the way home, even when Oliver grabbed her and kissed the top of her head and tried to get her to say "U Nork" again.

* * *

Rose was still very quiet later that evening when her family took the subway to Chinatown for dinner. It was Sunday night, and on Sundays they went down to Chinatown for Italian food. New York was like that: a Thai restaurant in a Dominican neighborhood, and Jewish pastrami sliced by Cambodian pastrami slicers.

Tonight, though, they had to wait in a long line outside The Arcade. While they waited, Oliver made Rose let him practice the "watch steal" on her. Oliver loved magic tricks. He was trying to learn how to do a watch steal—taking a watch from someone's wrist without the person noticing. The trick was to hold both wrists and sort of dance with them, so that the person was distracted, then slip the watchband off. But since Rose knew exactly what Oliver was going to do when he grasped her wrists, it was hard for her to feign distraction and surprise when Oliver stole her watch.

Their father sighed. He hated waiting in lines outside restaurants. "It's all the B and T people."

"He means 'bridge and tunnel' people," their mother explained to Rose. "All the out-of-town people who come into the city over bridges and through tunnels on a Sunday night."

"Oliver, now you have to teach me a magic trick. Remember?" Rose said. Oliver always promised that if she let him do the watch steal, and pretended to be distracted, he would teach her something.

"Okay," Oliver said. "I'll teach you how to do a Mercury fold." He always kept a deck of cards in the pocket of his leather jacket. (Rose wanted a leather jacket, too, but her mother said that it was too "tough girl," and that she looked pretty in her violet wool coat.) And he showed her a very complicated way of secretly folding up a single card on the bottom of the deck with one hand, while clutching the rest of the deck with the other.

"See? That way, you can slip the folded card under somebody's watch, or into someone's pocket or something," Oliver explained, "and they'll be amazed."

Rose tried practicing the Mercury fold while they waited in line. But the cards kept slipping from her hands. Folding the card secretly was too hard for her small fingers.

"It's just practice, Rosie," Oliver said kindly. "Okay, now let me try the watch steal again. . . ." And she had to let him grab her wrists and pretend to be surprised when he undid the clasp of her Swatch watch and slipped it off.

"If you live in New York, the prices we pay, you should go right to the front of the line," her father said moodily.

Rose knew that her father didn't really mean this, but that he sort of meant it, and that it was also part of his slightly misguided sense of humor. He was always complaining about how expensive New York was to raise children in and how easy it'd be to move to the suburbs. Though her mother always objected, and she knew her father was only joking, it still made Rose's heart jump with worry.

After dinner, which was delicious—Rose got to order her favorite, *penne amatriciana*—they decided to treat themselves to a taxi ride home, and that made Rose glad. Often the most intimate times her family had together in New York were when everyone piled into a taxi.

"Isn't it funny," Rose's mother said, "that you never ever ride with the same taxi driver twice in New York? At least, I never have."

Rose looked up as they crossed Twenty-third Street at First Avenue. The avenues of New York are straight, endless streets that run for hundreds of blocks, uptown and downtown, without a single swerve or curve or change. Every avenue was lined with brightly lit, two-story shops. Crossing Twenty-third Street, she saw a gym bright as day on the second floor of a building lined with wide glass windows. She could see all the grown-ups panting and pressing and sweating on their stationary bikes and treadmills, even though it was ten thirty at night. They looked as if they were on stage, although, given that they were all a bit chubby and perspiring, it couldn't have been a very good play.

"Dad," she asked, "why are they exercising? I mean, in the middle of the night and everything?"

Their father shrugged. "I suppose they're exercising in order to stay in good shape," he said.

"What will they be able do when they're in better shape?" she asked.

"More exercise," her mother answered dryly. Oliver snickered.

"It's weird to keep doing the same thing over and over forever with no real point," Rose said decisively.

"What do you mean? Why do you think I married your mother?" he said.

No one laughed. That misguided sense of humor of her dad's involved a lot of woeful puns and old jokes that hadn't really been funny the first time you heard them. But their mother smiled at them. She was the only one who did.

"But if everyone is exercising—why don't they look wonderfully fit?" their mother said suddenly. She was the sort of woman who would be serenely quiet for a long time and then suddenly burst out with a loud idea. "Do you see people looking wonderfully fit? I don't. It's the same question I have about clothes. Everywhere you look." She gestured at the avenue as the cab sped along and the cabdriver spoke in guttural language on his cell phone, laughing every few moments as though he and the person at the other end were exchanging very short, funny jokes. "Everywhere you look there are clothing stores selling beautiful clothes. But do you see everyone looking incredibly well dressed? Where are the people who wear all the beautiful clothes?"

Rose knew what was coming next, and she and Oliver both tightened up a little inside waiting for it.

"*You're* beautifully fit and beautifully dressed," their father said. "You take up all the space for it. The only one in New York who is."

Rose couldn't see her mother, but she knew that she was pleased. She and Oliver made faces at each other. It's nice when your parents flirt with each other, but not too much.

"As to why," their father said moodily, "you never get the same taxi driver twice in New York, I've got a theory about that. . . ."

As he spoke, Rose saw a long, gleaming, pink limousine pull up beside them, going north on Park Avenue. Car headlights momentarily lit up the limo's inside, right through its tinted windows. In the backseat Rose could make out a white fur collar and a pair of blazing amber eyes—like cat's eyes—with diamond-shaped irises.

"Rich people," Oliver said shortly. The pink limo had

caught his eye, too. "Or prep school kids going to clubs. They're the only ones with limousines." But Rose didn't think those eyes belonged to rich people. Or to prep school kids, either.

Later that evening, Rose watched as Oliver did his homework. He was studying astronomy in school and learning how, when a star dies, it becomes the most powerful radio transmitter in the universe, and also how, if it's big enough to collapse in on itself, it can become as dense and hard as a giant diamond.

"There's a white dwarf star in the constellation of Centaurus, next to the Southern Cross," Oliver said, "with a diamond at its core that weighs five million trillion trillion pounds."

Rose couldn't believe it. The idea of a diamond as big as a planet thrilled her. If she had a diamond that size she could—well, she would be rich. She could buy anything she wanted. Even a house to keep a dog of her own in.

When Rose was safe in bed, her father came in to tell her a bedtime story. Usually he told her a long story about the King of Central Park, an imaginary character he had made up. But tonight Rose wanted to hear another story.

"Tell me about the Princess of the Northern Snows," she said.

Her father looked surprised. "I haven't told you *that* one in a long time," he said.

"Please? I want to hear it tonight," Rose said simply.

So her father began telling her the long story that he had made up. "You were born far from us, Rose, dropped accidentally in the snows of Russia. But we knew that you belonged here in New York with us, so Mother and I made a long journey to the snow lands to find you. We searched and searched through the wastes and wind until we came upon a house made of ice. And inside was the most beautiful baby girl that had ever been seen. And we said, 'You are the child of the winter star, and you have been misplaced. Come home with us!' And the beautiful baby nodded her head to mean yes, and that's how the Princess of the Northern Snows came home with us to New York City."

Rose nodded sleepily. She knew it wasn't the exact truth—she had been adopted in Russia, and she could just barely remember the orphanage—but she loved the story. The Princess of the Winter Stars comes home. . . .

"Dad," she said suddenly, "I really did see steps across the water today in the park."

"I know you did, darling," he said. But she knew from the calm and detached way he said it that he didn't believe her.

Rose pretended to fall asleep, turning to the wall, breathing deeply and slowly in order to make her father feel that he had at last lulled her into slumber with his story. He couldn't see that her eyes stayed open. She tried to be sensitive to his feelings.

But the truth was, Rose was frightened. She often had strange, scary dreams. She sometimes had a nightmare where she was falling, falling from a high place. And sometimes she had nightmares about Rumpelstiltskin, the evil dwarf who taunted the young queen. But tonight she thought mostly of the steps across the water, about how strange and beautiful they had seemed, and how quickly they had come and gone. For comfort, she looked at the bulletin board on the wall by her bed, where she'd tacked up photographs of dogs she wished she owned. But even thinking about a dog didn't cheer Rose up.

She got out of bed and tiptoed to her window. Oliver had told her of his own adventures once with a strange figure who appeared in the window. But tonight there was nothing there.

Had Rose looked more closely, though—had she leaned right over the sill and looked down six stories to the street— she would have seen the four tiny figures, no bigger than kindergartners, talking in deep, gravelly, rumbling voices and looking up at her window.

She would have seen the pink limousine pull up, too— one of the long, extended kind, as long as two regular cars—and the four figures, glancing all around, walk hurriedly away, in different directions across the city.

Although Rose couldn't see these things, something inside told her something strange was happening. She could feel it. The October wind, which had begun to quicken in the park as evening fell, was wild now and whistling through the windows.

Rose ran down the hall clutching her blanket. Her parents' door was shut tight, and she couldn't get in. She thought of pounding on the door but then thought better of it.

Instead she crept into Oliver's room and made herself a bed on the floor out of covers and her pillow. Oliver didn't notice. Once he was asleep, he was really asleep. The music he listened to, to help him fall asleep, was still playing. Rose lay awake, her large eyes wide open, and waited for morning. *Who am I,* she whispered into the surroundings, *and where do I really come from?* If I knew where I came from, I'd know who I am. And if I had a dog, I wouldn't be lonely.

And what did I really see in the park today?

But no one answered. Or even barked. At least, not yet.

Chapter Two

THE BUDDY SYSTEM

Rose went to a "progressive" school, which meant, said her father, "that they're progressively draining my bank account. . . ." He stood in the doorway of Rose's room, with his hoodie and sweatpants on, at seven thirty in the morning, gulping his coffee. Rose's mother was in Rose's bedroom, carefully braiding Rose's long hair.

"Don't drink so much caffeine," her mother said. "It isn't good for you."

"If it weren't for coffee and e-mail, I wouldn't know I was alive," he said, turning to walk to the kitchen.

What a progressive school really meant was that, while kids at other schools studied reading, writing, and arithmetic, Rose was taking class trips to famous landmarks and writing poems about them. The week before, her class had walked across the Brooklyn Bridge and written poems about it in the style of the great Walt Whitman. "O Mighty Bridge," Rose's had begun. "O flocks of seagulls filling my eyes." Chloe, the meanest kid in the grade, had made fun of her. "O flocks of seagulls pooping on my head."

That was the kind of thing that happened to Rose all the time.

When her mother fastened Rose's braid with a pink ribbon, she caught a glimpse of Rose's face in the mirror. "What's wrong, darling?"

She somehow knew when Rose was worried, as mothers always did.

"We're studying the Empire State Building in school all week," Rose said gloomily. "So today we have to do a show-and-tell about some aspect of it in the afternoon, and tomorrow we have to go to it. Then the day after that we have off, and then we have to write a poem about what we saw."

"Well, what's wrong with that?"

"It's boring," Rose said. "Who cares how they made it just to be taller than the Chrysler Building?"

"I bet Mr. Chrysler cared," her mother said. "Anyway, show-and-tell is fun."

"Show is fun. Tell is fun. Together they're boring," Rose said, ever gloomier. "But it's not just that. I'm worried about the . . ."

"What, darling?"

"You know. Saying the words reversed," she muttered.

"Oh. That's nothing, darling. First of all, it won't happen. And even if it did, there's nothing wrong with it. Everybody does something like that. When I was your age, I lisped."

"Lisps are cute," Rose objected. "Saying words reversed is weird. Kids laugh."

"I'm sure the teacher won't let them laugh. I'm sure it won't even happen. It happened when you were small, because you were so eager to get the words out. Never was there a better talker than you. Now, get your backpack and head to the kitchen. Dad's making you waffles."

Rose was going to say that she had outgrown waffles, but she didn't. She actually liked them.

"It'll be okay, my love," her mother said as she made her way toward the door. "Trust me. Just trust me."

"Excited for your big day at school today, Partly?" her father asked as he walked her to school. He liked calling her "Partly" because one of her classmates was named "Stormy." It had been raining the night her friend was born, and her parents had wanted to remember that fact. "If we had followed the same principle," Rose's father liked to say, "then you might have been called something like 'Partly Cloudy with a Chance of Showers.' And just 'Partly' for short."

Of course, Rose knew that her father didn't really know what the weather had been like the night she was born, and that he was trying to make her feel more "normal" by pretending that he did. It was also true that the kids in her class often had odd names. There was Stormy and Summer-Song, even a boy named Angle.

"Dad . . ." Rose said.

"What?" her father asked.

"You know."

"No, sweetie. I'm not sure I follow."

"I hate school," Rose said.

Rose, of course, didn't really hate her school, but sometimes she could only get her parents' attention by exaggerating her emotions.

"How can you hate school? You do so many wonderful things there. Don't you enjoy doing interpretive dances of Orpheus and Eurydice to the music of John Coltrane?" he asked. That's what they did in school when they weren't going to the Brooklyn Bridge or the Empire State Building and writing poems about them.

"I just do," Rose said. "I hate it. I think all the other kids hate me."

"Nobody could hate you. Just as you don't hate them,"

her father objected. "You just don't love them. Sometimes you just have to struggle with people you're supposed to love but don't really like. That's part of life."

"Fine. But I hate it."

The truth, though, was that Rose didn't really hate her school, and especially not her teacher, Ms. Elizabeth Elder. She thought she was actually quite interesting when she talked about Greek myths, and even nice at times, when she talked about the history of jazz.

"She's cold," Rose insisted.

"Well, maybe Ms. Elder doesn't have warmth, but does she have heart?"

"What's the difference?"

"Someone with warmth shows their affection. Someone with heart appreciates life, but doesn't always show it. You know what's more important than heart or warmth?"

"What?"

"Soul. Someone with soul. And do you know what's more important than soul?"

"What, Dad?"

"Money," he answered moodily. "Which we don't got, Rosebud. But which do you really think is most important?"

Rose sensed that her father was exaggerating his emotions in the same way that she exaggerated hers. They both used the morning walk as an opportunity to vent their feelings in the gloomiest possible way. It was sort of understood between them. So now she made a little joke to let her father know that she knew that he was joking.

"The ones with the fewest syllables," she said.

He laughed. "Good answer. Look at the mannequin in the window! She's bursting her gussets."

Every morning they walked by a clothes store with one very large mannequin in the window.

"Hey, kiddo," her father said quickly, and Rose knew that he was thinking about what her mother would say. "I don't want you to get the impression that it's important for women to be thin. You know—whatever weight . . ."

"*Dad.* I know," Rose said. She could sometimes say her dad's name the way that Oliver said hers. It was funny, she thought—the thing about someone being in the same family was that you knew when they were sort of joking, when they were sort of serious, when they were truly serious, and when they said one thing but were thinking of something else—the way that her father must have been thinking of her mother when he said that thing about women being fat.

"You know, Dad," she said, trying to express this as best she could, "it's actually sort of appropriate that you would call me 'Partly,' because we each *partly* understand *all* of what the other one is thinking."

Her father actually stopped walking when she said that, and took her by the hand and said quietly, in that goopy way grown-ups often have, "Rosie! I'll think about that all day. Or part of it, at least."

When they got to school, Rose went upstairs to her classroom. Someone tugged at her sleeve.

It was little Ethan, the smallest, sweetest, but also the saddest kid in the grade. Ethan had those big moist eyes and a small runny nose that he was always wiping on his mittens. He sort of looked up to Rose—he was pretty much the only one in her class who did—and so Rose tried always to be kind to him, even when he was being annoying, which he once again was now.

"Rose," he said shyly, "I'm worried about going so high up in the Empire State Building. Will we be using the buddy system?"

"No, Ethan," she sighed. "We won't be using the buddy system. That's for when you're at summer camp and you can get lost in the woods. . . ."

"But I could get lost so high up. Please be my buddy, Rose?"

"It's only, like, fifteen feet from the door to the observation deck. It's nothing. You'll be fine."

But Ethan only looked up at her again with his big sad eyes, so Rose sighed again and said, "Okay, Ethan. I'll be your buddy." She had the nice, small reward of seeing him smile with contentment.

Actually, Ethan was okay, she supposed, walking to her locker. He was the only kid in class who really understood about her wanting a dog. He wanted one, too—only in his case he was the one with the allergies—and sometimes he and Rose would sit in the back of the class and silently trade pictures of beautiful, charming Havanese puppies. They were her favorite breed. "I'm sure you'll get a dog of your own someday, Rose," he had said solemnly, just the day before.

And compared to some of the other kids in her class— like Eloise, for instance, who Rose just realized was standing by her locker, waiting for her—Ethan was actually almost great. Sniffles and all.

Rose approached Eloise cautiously.

"Don't forget we're going to look at snow globes for our collections this afternoon," Eloise said loudly, so that their teacher, Ms. Elder, would hear and think that it was a warm invitation. It sounded to Rose more like a subtle but mean taunt. The way she said "our collections" reminded Rose how small her collection was, while Eloise's was quite big—which, Rose knew, was the whole idea.

The rest of the morning didn't go much better, but nothing went really drastically wrong. During recess she tried to play basketball with Seth, Eliot, and Dylan on the roof, but even though they let her shoot a little (Ms. Elder would have lectured them if they hadn't, for not being Caring enough), she could tell that they were just waiting for her to finish so they could go back to their own game.

Morning Meeting, Community Commons, Something Done for Others Time, and the Sharing, Caring Circle were all fine too, if a little goopy.

But then came the part of the day that Rose was really dreading. She had to give her report on the Empire State Building.

It started off okay; she began explaining how all of the builders in Manhattan in the 1930s had competed to build the highest skyscraper. People liked very high buildings in those days, she explained. They would even moor blimps and zeppelins to their very highest points. But then exactly what she was scared of happened. She was planning to say, "The Empire State Building is now the highest building in New York . . ." and instead it came out, "The Empire State Building is now the highest building in U Nork. . . ."

And everyone laughed. They tried to turn it into laughing with her (because Ms. Elder gave them all a look), but Rose knew that they were really laughing at her. She shot a look at her classmates. Eloise and Wendy were both laughing into their hands, sort of showing off that they were politely not laughing at her while actually laughing at her. The other kids chuckled, and then caught themselves. Only little Ethan didn't laugh at all—and even he looked at her with a strange, opaque, mysterious and worried look, as though she had said something that wasn't funny at all.

When school finally ended, she tried to feel cheerful about going with Eloise to Madame Raines's, the snow globe store over on Second Avenue, even though Eloise had laughed harder than anyone. Rose sighed; she tried so hard to be liked and to like the other kids, but she never for a minute felt that she belonged. Well—Rose wanted to be precise—she felt that she belonged for a minute, but never for more than a minute. That was the problem.

Eloise was very rich, lived on Park Avenue, and always acted quietly superior in a way that fooled you about how nice she was, because she wasn't. Eloise and Rose hardly talked, but a couple of weeks ago Rose had mentioned how much she loved snow globes, and Eloise overheard. Eloise opened her eyes wide and raised her eyebrows—a very annoying habit she had—and said, with pretend niceness, that Rose ought to see *her* collection of snow globes. Rose knew she should say no—Eloise was always saying mean things about her other friends, so she was also certainly saying mean things about Rose—but she couldn't resist; Rose loved snow globes that much.

She loved how the little glass domes filled with water had models of city skylines or country scenes inside them, and when you turned them over, little bits of confetti filled the water to make it look like it was snowing. Rose had one snow globe from Paris, where her parents had taken her, and another from Seattle, Washington, which her father had brought home for her from a business trip. It had the Space Needle in it.

So Rose had gone over to Eloise's house—the apartment on Park Avenue—only to realize too late that Eloise had invited her just to make her feel bad. Eloise had about six million snow globes, all of them big and lined up on a shelf with a light underneath, so that they glowed when she turned the switch. Eloise wouldn't even let Rose shake them up because they were too fragile.

Rose felt a little sick and inferior seeing Eloise's snow globes, which she knew had been the whole idea. Then Eloise said: "You know, the best snow globe store in New York is on Second Avenue at Eighty-fifth Street. Let's go there together after school one day."

Again, Rose knew she should resist. Eloise only ever made her feel bad. "I, uh, better ask my mom," Rose said, stalling.

"Don't be such a bore. We're older now. Didn't you

get the memo?" Eloise always said, "Didn't you get the memo?" if something was passé.

"Well, they'll be worried if they don't know where I am."

"They can always call you on your cell," Eloise said, with a showy shake of her head.

"I haven't got a cell," Rose said.

"Oh!" Eloise said. She seemed to make a point of not raising her eyebrows and looking surprised, as if she realized, for once, that she shouldn't hurt Rose's feelings on purpose, which was almost more annoying than if she had. "Well, here's what we'll do. You tell your mom that you're going to my house, and I'll tell my babysitter that I'm going to yours, and then we'll go to Madame Raines's. That's the snow globe store."

"I shouldn't lie to my parents," Rose said.

"They'll be proud of you," Eloise said, "for showing initiative. You're going forth unafraid." That was the motto of their school.

Rose did *love* snow globes. . . .

So, after school that day, Rose found herself alongside her frenemy, about to head to the snow globe store. She had felt really worried after telling her mom that she was going home with Eloise—the school made her parents sign a form saying it was okay—but Eloise said airily that her mother didn't care, one way or another, which made Rose imagine that Eloise could be gone from home for weeks before anyone noticed (Eloise's mom was nice, but always busy). If Rose was fifteen minutes late, her mom and dad looked as if they were going to commit suicide.

For once, as the girls headed to the snow globe shop, to Rose's great relief Eloise didn't look superior or condescending. She just looked excited.

Madame Raines's turned out to be one of those stores in the basement of an old apartment building. You had to walk down three steps to reach it.

The sign outside just said ANTIQUES. It wasn't the kind of store Eloise usually liked. She liked cool places, like Dylan's Candy Bar, the expensive jellybean store. Not places like this—a store with a lot of dust and old furniture crowded together on an old rug.

A man with long white hair and a strange expression stood behind the counter.

"Careful not to touch anything," he said, with a twisted smile on his lips. "Of course, it's more touching not to care for anything. Freedom lies in that," he said mysteriously.

Eloise ignored him and led Rose around old rocking chairs and mirrors. There they were: a locked glass case full of snow globes.

Rose got on her knees and looked at them with

fascination. Some looked very old, like the ones showing miniature scenes from old World's Fairs, with monorails intersecting tall, white pyramid pavilions, or ocean liners crossing the ocean and planes cutting across the sky. Some showed Paris with the Eiffel Tower, and some showed New York and the Empire State Building.

High on a shelf by themselves was a set of six larger snow globes, each nearly the size of a crystal ball. Rose could hardly see into them, but they seemed to show scenes from imaginary cities. One city in particular looked modern in an old-fashioned way, like it was from the nineteen thirties—filled with skyscrapers with funny, decorated tops like the Chrysler Building, and monorails running through them, and dirigibles overhead. Rose wondered what city it was. She wished she could open the cabinet, give the globes a shake, and watch the snow fall on the strange city.

"If you break it you own it. Of course, if you own it, you *will* break it, sooner or later. It's a rule of life," a strange, whispering voice said. It was the man behind the counter. He had come around and was standing near the kneeling girls.

"Who's that?" Rose whispered to Eloise.

"That's Madame Raines's assistant, Mr. Wiselholtz. He's so random. He always says sentences in reverse."

Rose didn't say anything. The man stood behind them and breathed, hard.

"I can show you the snow on the city," a kinder voice said. Rose turned around to find a frail-looking woman with white hair piled on her head. She had a fluty voice and a strange, unsteady gaze. "Do you want to see the snow on the city, dear?"

"Yes," Rose said, a little shakily herself. The woman must've been Madame Raines.

"Do you want me to shake them?" Madame Raines said, almost greedily.

"Yes, please," Rose repeated.

The white-haired woman took a key from around her throat and opened the glass case. She carefully mounted a step ladder, took one of the old globes of New York from the cabinet's third shelf, and, very gently, turned it over, then right side up.

It was beautiful! Snow fell gently all around the city, over the Chrysler Building and the water towers. And, where usually in snow globes the snow settles quickly, in this globe the snow somehow kept falling, gently, as if it was real snow falling from the sky, not just bits of tiny confetti that had to be shaken from the bottom.

"How does it—" Rose began.

"How does the snow keep falling?" Madame Raines

said. "Ah! That's a secret of the workmanship! The cheap kind—the airport kind arc made with shredded paper." The old woman shuddered at the thought. "The collector's snow globes are made with—well, a more exquisite touch. They will keep snowing . . . as long as you like."

The two girls stared into the beautiful, soft-snowing globe.

Suddenly, Eloise spoke up. "How much?"

Madame Raines and Mr. Wiselholtz looked at her as though they were stunned.

"Oh, child," Madame Raines said, "it's far more than you can afford."

"If you have to ask, you can't afford it," Mr. Wiselholtz added. "And if you can afford it, you'd be too rich to ask."

Eloise was too stubborn to take a hint.

"My father . . ." she began.

While she spoke, Rose realized that Madame Raines had left the ladder outside the cabinet. While they were busy with Eloise, Rose climbed the ladder and stole a quick look inside the biggest of the snow globes. It was like looking down on a whole city.

It reminded her of one her father had bought for her, the one that showed all the monuments of New York— the Guggenheim Museum, with its white spiral, and Bloomingdale's, the department store, thin and tall. Only this globe was even bigger and better, and its glass shell gleamed, bright and crystalline. Rose stared inside, trying to pick out the monuments and decide which city it was supposed to be—she knew that the Saks Fifth Avenue chain had once made snow globes of all the great cities of America, and she supposed that it must be one of those. Was that Chicago? The super-tall tower . . .

But just as she was beginning to speculate happily, Madame Raines saw her and strode over quickly to shut the cabinet. The spell was broken. Rose looked down. The snow had even stopped in the snow globe.

Rose climbed down the ladder and looked longingly at the closed cabinet.

"Oh," she said, "I was so hoping to see the big ones!"

"The big ones?" Madame Raines said. "You mean those?" She pointed toward the large snow globes of the city that Rose had been looking at. "Oh, I can't show you those. Not yet, dear. Those are only shaken once in a great while for the people who own them. Someday, perhaps, when you're more of a . . . collector."

"Well, I want to buy them. I'll bring my dad," said Eloise. Rose knew that Eloise was being obnoxious, but she kind of admired her spirit.

"Girls who are so certain," said Madame Raines dryly, "find themselves in trouble, more often than not." But then she was smiling. "Come, girls. I have just the thing for you."

Madame Raines led them over to the case by the cash register. There were many smaller snow globes there, showing scenes of Central Park in winter. Eloise and Rose each chose one. Eloise took one with the skating rink, with kids all over and the New York skyline all around.

Rose chose one that she thought was even more beautiful. It showed a carriage drawn by two horses with two children inside, riding through Central Park at night. The carriage was about to pass under a snow-covered bridge and there was a moon behind them, held up by a tiny wire, and a streetlamp nearby, which even had a little bulb in it painted yellow, so you could tell that it was night. Rose thought that it was the most beautiful thing that she had ever seen. She imagined the children were she and Oliver, riding in the carriage, behind the driver with his whip and the two palomino horses.

Eloise and Rose paid for them—each one cost fifteen dollars, which was all the money Rose had saved up. Eloise paid with a credit card, and then they left the store.

"Come back soon," Madame Raines called after them.

"Those who come back soon," her assistant added, "soon come back."

The two girls walked back out onto the street.

"Let's look at them," Eloise urged.

"Shouldn't we wait until we're home?"

But Eloise insisted, so they sat down on a stoop—that's what front steps are called in New York City—and opened their shopping bags.

"Mine's the most beautiful," Eloise said obnoxiously.

Annoyed, Rose lifted hers high up in her two hands.

"I like mine," she said. "Like the way you can see the moon in it and—amah—no!"

The snow globe had slipped between her woolen gloves and broke to pieces on the pavement.

Even Eloise was silent. Tears welled up in Rose's eyes. She bent down, wishing she could turn the moment back. The snow globe lay shattered, a hundred fragments of glass, and the water inside had all flowed out and puddled on the ground.

All the beautiful miniature figures—the children and the horses and the moon—lay tumbled out and broken on the sidewalk. Rose reached down to pick up the little carriage where the two children were riding under the cozy checked blanket. She held the two figures up and didn't know what to do with them.

Then, to make it worse, she saw that the girl had had a tiny white dog on her lap, hidden under the blanket. She'd had a dog, all along. It was perfect, and now it was ruined forever.

Rose put the three figures of the girl and boy and dog into her pocket. She reached down, fighting back tears, to see if she could save any more of the pieces.

"It's okay, Rose," Eloise said. She was actually trying to be nice. "We can get you another one next week."

Rose turned her back on Eloise and ran home, the pieces of her shattered snow globe in her pocket.

The next afternoon, on the bus to the Empire State Building, Ethan kept his big liquid eyes fixed on her, and when they got off the bus at Fifth Avenue and Thirty-fourth Street, he came up to her and said, "Remember! You promised to be my buddy in the buddy system!"

"Ethan, there is no buddy system. There are no buddies—" Rose started to say. Then she sighed and gave up. If he wanted a buddy, she'd be his buddy. She had promised.

A few minutes later, the whole class was at the top of the Empire State Building. It was freezing cold and all the kids were huddled round the edge, looking out over the great city from so high above. You could see the tops of all the buildings and look right down on them. You could even see the water towers and heating fans too. It was scary. Central Park looked like a big flat green envelope right in the middle of the city. Stormy took out a map and started drawing where each thing was. Stormy, the closest person

she had to a best friend, was working on the map as-
signment too. It was cold and boring and the wind blew
hard.

All last night Rose had thought about her snow globe.
The way it had looked the instant after it had broken—
so . . . *ruined*, with the little figures lying on the ground,
and the snow and water all around.

She just couldn't bear to think about it, but she couldn't
stop thinking about it either.

Rose walked around the corner of the observation deck
to see what was happening on the building's north side.
There was Ethan, all alone.

"Hello, Ethan," she said, and he looked so wistful that
she added, as warmly as she could, "Hey there, buddy!"

He looked pleased. "Hey, buddy!" he echoed, in a
sweet, innocent voice. Then Rose heard a strange sound,
like flapping wings, somewhere near the building, and she
turned her head to look for it.

And then she heard Ethan repeat himself, only he
must have caught something in his throat, because now it
sounded sort of raspy: "Hey, buddy!"

"Is something wrong, Ethan?" Rose asked, still facing
away from him.

"Hey, Rosie, I hear ya'wanna go to U Nork," Ethan
said, only now his voice was *really* low and growly and weird.

Rose quickly turned back to face him. It looked like he had a cigar planted between his teeth.

Rose blinked. Little Ethan really was smoking a cigar! Smoke came out of the fiery end. He took the cigar from his mouth and blew a ring at her.

"Ain't that right, sweetheart?" he asked.

It was Ethan's mouth moving, that was for certain, but it didn't sound a bit like him. He sounded like . . . a gangster, or something.

"Next stop, U Nork," he said, and spit out a bit of cigar ash.

"Ethan?" Rose said weakly.

"My name ain't Ethan. Or Owen, or Dylan, or Elijah, or Rainy Day, or any of them sissy names, see?" He took a big drag on his cigar. "The name's Louis, see? Pronounced Looey, like a guy, not Loo-ees, like a French guy. Ya got that, sugartoes? It's Louis. And I'm supposed to find out what you know about U Nork, and which bridge you wanna take to get there, see? The mayeh sent me."

"Ethan." Rose looked over her shoulder to see if Stormy or somebody was nearby. But there was no one there . . . Wait, Dylan and Seth were coming round. Rose breathed a little easier. It was weird being stuck here with Ethan, or Louis, or whoever he was. . . .

Then she realized, as Dylan and Seth gathered around

Louis, that they were smoking cigars too.

"Yeah, that's right, sweetheart. Now listen, we ain't got all day! Where did you hear about the big game and the big town, and can you help us?"

"What game, what town? *This* is the big town."

"*This is the big town.* You hear that, Mack and Charlie? Fellas, this lady calls this little burg the big town." And they all laughed deep big laughs. "Why, it's the—"

"Ethan! Why are you talking like that?"

"What do you mean, 'Talking like that'? The other way is phony, sugartoes. I'm a midget, see, not a kid. Every classroom in this little town has a midget among the children. We gotta watch stuff, see. Figure out who's on to us and who isn't. I'm like ya guardian angel, see? Ya buddy, like I said." All three of them laughed at that. "Only I'm really an observant midget."

"You're a midget? From where?"

"From the big town, obviously . . . It's a hell of a life for a midget, being stuck forever in the fourth grade . . . I got multiplication tables comin' out my ears by now."

"Why do you—"

"Well, someone's gotta— Wait? Did ja hear that?"

Rose heard a rumble like a car.

"She must be on to us! Look down quick, Rosie-toes, and see what you see."

Rose got up on tiptoes and looked down the side of the building. She blinked. It couldn't be . . . but it was. A pink limousine—the same one that she'd seen on the street the night before. But now it was . . . racing up the side of the skyscraper, like a car on a slot.

"Yikes—it's her! We gotta go. But remember, Rose: if you wanna go there, be at the steps across the water at twilight. The big steps. You know—around quarter of seven, and find me on the other side. The mayeh wants to have breakfast with you."

"Wait, where—why?"

"You'll find out when you get there. Just do it! Listen. If you come over the steps, you'll get a dog. Of your own."

"A dog!" Of course; Ethan—or whatever his name really was—knew all about that. Then she thought of something. "I can't. My mom's allergic. You know."

But the midget just laughed. "Hey, kid, the kind of dog I got in mind, believe me, it ain't allergic to anyone. It goes wherever it likes and welcomes whoever it meets!"

Rose thought of something else.

"Can I get a snow globe, too?" she asked.

Louis looked puzzled for a moment. "You mean one of those toy things you turn over so it snows?" Then he shrugged. A sly smile spread across his face. "Yeah. You can get a snow globe. A big and beautiful one. For sure."

Rose was a little suspicious. "That's it?" she said. "I just go over those steps, and then I have breakfast with the mayor and get my dog and a new snow globe?" She wanted Louis to know that she hadn't fallen off a turnip truck that morning.

"Well, of course, first, you gotta save the whole—" Louis began reasonably. But before he could complete his sentence, Ethan and Dylan and Seth—or Louis and Mack and Charlie—did something astounding. They crouched down low, like a gymnastics team, and vaulted themselves, in a single backward somersault, above the parapet and fence and right out off the Empire State Building.

Rose gasped in fear. They were falling! She raced to the edge of the building.

"No!" she cried.

The three small boys—or weird little midget men—were falling like skydivers without a parachute. Down they fell, and Rose's heart flew up to her mouth. She could feel their falling in the pit of her stomach. She could sense their terror as they plummeted down through the cold air, while the granite building flew by, and the ground below rose up so quickly. . . .

Suddenly, three giant gray birds (like pigeons, only the size of ponies) swept into view from out of the clouds behind the Empire State Building. Each one wore a bridle of gold and a red leather saddle, right on the middle of its back.

The three boys continued to fall, and the three giant gray birds flew just beneath them. *Plop*—each boy landed on a pigeon's back and grabbed hold of the bridle around its neck. Then the pigeons flapped their wings mightily and took off. The pink limousine stopped just at the edge of the observation tower, and like a Hot Wheel on its track, reversed down, in a single *whoosh,* in the opposite direction. Rose leaned over to see what was happening. The entire limousine was heading straight for the ground—but seconds before it struck, the pavement itself opened up, swallowed the speeding car, and closed again.

Rose turned back and scanned the sky, but everything had already disappeared, giant pigeons and midgets alike. Suddenly, Rose felt cold. On the floor of the observation deck, a giant winged shadow, like that of a hawk, passed above the building.

She felt very cold indeed.

Chapter Three

IN THE CITY

That night, Rose knew she had to do something brave; she had to go into Central Park at twilight and look for the steps across the water. How could she not at least try? After all, the strange midgets must have picked *her* out of all the kids in class for a reason. Maybe it was with them, on this adventure that she belonged, Rose thought.

She couldn't just put everything behind her and pretend it hadn't happened just because she was scared.

But she *was* scared. In books, she reminded herself, children often did extremely courageous things—but then they never seem to be scared in the first place. They shut their eyes, summoned up the courage, and did brave things. In real life, though, being brave was hard. Even simple, everyday brave things were hard for her. She'd once tried to walk past an angry German shepherd tied up in front of their neighborhood supermarket. Even though the dog had only been barking—and even though she really loved dogs—Rose found that when it bared its teeth and barked, her body began to tremble and her legs locked in place.

So when Rose went out at twilight to the bridge in the park, she was not stepping forward bravely, or with secret excitement. She was scared, and she had to force her body forward. But she was ready to go ahead and do it at the chance of a dog.

Before she left, she had tried telling Oliver what had happened.

"Oliver, I saw three kids today, only they were really midgets and they—"

But Oliver had just ignored her. "Sure, Rose. Whatever," he said, and turned back to his computer screen, where he was IMing friends. It infuriated her. Oliver, she knew, had once had an adventure with some very odd people in very strange places—she had heard him talk about it—but anything odd and interesting that happened to her was just . . . "Whatever."

"Whatever" indeed! She would just have to find out where the steps led for herself.

So after her parents left for a dinner party, and Oliver was plugged into his headphones—lost to his computer—Rose slipped into her best coat, the violet coat her mother had bought for her at the French clothing store on Madison, put on a pink woolen hat, and went back to the park to find the steps across the water. If she hurried, she'd be back before her parents got home.

Rose had almost never been away from home by herself. She had never crossed many streets by herself. And now she was walking on her own into Central Park at nightfall, to see where the steps would lead. Did she really want to do this? she wondered as she stole through the city. It was all so weird, she thought: boys who turned out to be midgets and rode giant pigeons. . . . Even if she wasn't imagining it—and she was sure she wasn't—did she want to be part of something so strange and scary? Sure, she liked stories about kids who went to strange countries; but they were mostly enchanting. What if she was going somewhere that was just plain freaky?

But a dog of her own . . . and a snow globe to replace the one that had broken . . . especially if Louis was being truthful about its being a dog that could go anywhere with anyone! And the chance to prove how serious and grownup she was!

Rose decided she would at least go and see if the steps were still there, and then make up her mind. She wouldn't do anything that seemed too weird or dangerous. She would just . . . check and make sure the steps were there, across the water. Then she would decide what to do next.

So in her violet coat she walked through the Children's Gate, the park entrance near Seventy-fifth Street. By now, the autumn evening had turned cold and the park lamps had been lit. They cast little pools of light before her feet. She was a tiny figure against the dark. Rose wished she could turn south, toward the Children's Zoo and the wonderful Delacorte Musical Clock, where a frieze of mechanical toy animals—bears, lions, and kangaroos— played musical instruments, dancing around the clock every hour on the hour. Nothing made Rose happier than watching the Delacorte Clock with Oliver. But she had another place to go this evening.

The park wasn't exactly empty—no place in New York is ever really completely empty—but was filled with what Rose called occasional people, who wrapped their coats tight around them as they walked their dogs in the autumn wind. She walked beneath the bridges where, in fine weather, flute players played and picnickers sat. At last Rose reached the Great Lawn, under the Castle, and she stared at the pond.

Nothing. Nothing at all. No glass steps, no small people. Just the cold breeze blowing across it.

Maybe she had imagined it.

"I can't say abracadabra, because it's so cheesy," she said. "Or presto, or anything." She sighed. Now she would have to go home again, and if they heard her sneaking in, they would really go nutty.

"Someday I'll go home to a place where everyone takes me seriously," she said to herself. "A place where I'll belong. Where I won't be the baby, or say stuff funny ways, and where everyone I meet will be my true friend and like me for who I am. And where I'll have a dog," she said. "Because I *want* a dog . . ."

And just like that, the steps appeared.

High and glass, reaching up into the air and then gracefully bending over the pond, the steps sparkled brightly even in the fading, slanting moonlight, as though they were lit from within. Dazzling her eyes, they led her—who knew where?

Clutching her courage as tightly to her as a dog on a leash, Rose walked across the steps. They were light under her feet, making sweet, musical tinkling noises as she crossed them, as though they were the keys on a glass xylophone. A bright light gleamed at the far end, and so she shut her eyes as she approached it, hearing the bright sounds of the glass steps beneath her slippers. . . .

The dry thud of firm ground beneath her feet at the other end made Rose open her eyes.

She seemed to be standing at the corner of Thirty-fourth

and Fifth Avenue, where she'd been that morning; the building above her looked like the Empire State Building. Rose was disappointed. Even a little puzzled.

But as she looked more carefully, and her dazzled eyes grew accustomed to the sunlight, she saw that she was actually in another, *different* city. The skyscrapers rose taller and taller, a mile high, right into the clouds above her, at least three times as tall as the Empire State Building. There were six, no, seven buildings, crowded on the single block on all four sides, each one taller than the next, and with strange tops: one had a figure of a fat man; the next, a man staring boldly toward the distant horizon, hand across his brow.

Open-sided cars went along the street, then turned abruptly up the faces of the buildings, like little bugs scooting up to the sky. Some of the buildings had slanting sides that the cars hooked onto and slowly climbed to the clouds above. Others had sides as straight as the ones on the buildings back home. On those, Rose saw that the drivers and passengers strapped themselves in before mounting and rocketing up, though one crazy-looking teenager had left his car open and was hooting all the way until he was lost from view.

Old-fashioned balloons—zeppelins and dirigibles—filled the sky, their gondolas swaying underneath. Squinting her eyes, Rose could make out in the low-flying balloons that people were reading newspapers and holding on to poles or carrying packages, just like on the subway back in New York. With a hand above her eyes to protect them from the sun, Rose strained to look even higher. The sun had a strange, bulbous shape in the sky and shone brightly here, she thought, though its light was somehow white rather than yellow.

And, darting around the flying balloons, giant pigeons flapped their wings, either pulling little carriages behind them or carrying people on their backs. She wondered if Louis was one of those passengers. How was she ever supposed to find him in this giant city?

Rose looked around the street where she'd arrived. So *many* people! They rushed along, whooshing down the pavement, twice or three times as fast as people at home. She realized they all had wheels on their shoes and were skating, not walking, in long, preoccupied strides. Rose had never seen so many beautifully dressed men and women! The men all wore two-piece suits, with narrow ties and dented, large-brimmed hats; the ladies all wore dresses with tight waists and long, flaring skirts, and high heels, and black hats with small crowns and wide brims. Rose wished her mother could see it; she'd be very pleased. . . .

"This way to the elevators?" a woman's voice asked, hard and shrill.

Rose shrugged.

"Well, didn't you just get off the elevator, kid? You look all mussed from a big trip."

The woman who'd spoken was part of a family. Beside her, her husband (Rose guessed) was holding six bags: three family bags, one duffel bag, and a baby carrier with a baby in it. He was perspiring very hard. Behind him, two older children, also loaded with suitcases, were sucking on giant lollipops. They looked sweaty, too. Everyone was walking as fast as they could, wrestling forward with their luggage. Curious, Rose followed.

"Here we are!" the woman said, and the family practically limped together into the building, as though they were worn out from traveling before the trip had even started. "If you're not going, you coming?" she called to Rose.

Rose stammered, "I—I guess so."

Rose followed them inside the building to its enormous lobby, many stories high and covered with marble, and into an open elevator. One by one, they sat down on the little jump seats and stowed their baggage underneath.

"We're going to the three thousandth floor, sir," the mother announced before realizing an elevator attendant was nowhere in sight. Her son groaned.

Rose was sure the woman had made some mistake . . .

but there, where the floor buttons always were, were the numbers . . . and they went up, all the way up, higher and higher: thousands of tiny buttons for thousands of floors.

"Another delay!" the mother cried.

The family started fanning each other.

"Oh, here's the operator," the father said.

A smartly dressed man in uniform got on the elevator. He saluted Rose with his cap, then turned to the buttons.

"Top floor, please," the mother said.

"On our way to the three thousandth floor . . . just about to close the doors . . ." he said, in a calm, drowsy voice. "Expected travel time of approximately eight hours . . ."

Eight hours! Rose didn't want to spend eight hours on an elevator! Not when she'd just arrived. She darted for the elevator doors just as they were closing and slipped back into the lobby, then back onto the sun-dazzled street.

People walked past her, their heads down, their feet barely touching the ground in their hurry. The crowd pulled her along the bright, broad pavement. Rose felt the warm, almost musty press of the grown-ups' woolen coats and the rich, heavy smell of women's perfume. She sniffed. Funny, it was a good smell—like lime mixed with the smell of frying bacon mixed with the smell of violets. She had never smelled it before.

The movement of the pedestrians pulled her toward a huge mezzanine, bordered by buildings, where a crowd gathered. It looked a lot like Rockefeller Center, in New York, where the Christmas tree is lit every year. In fact, as the crowd in front of her cleared a bit, she glimpsed that this square also had a giant Christmas tree and a glistening ice skating rink. Only—Rose blinked. The tree was upside down! The tip was planted in the ground, and the branches flared out from the trunk, which reached to the sky. Rose was sure even Eloise had never seen a forty-foot-tall Christmas tree balanced on the wrong end!

Rose fought her way through the crowd, pressing closer to the edge of the mezzanine. Someone—he must have been an official of the city, because he had a kind of old-fashioned chain around his neck—was making a speech. Could that be the mayor? She was supposed to have break-fast with him . . . though it seemed like mid-afternoon now in this strange city.

Rose couldn't follow the words the speaker was saying— they were coming over one of those public address systems that echo and distort every sound—but she could guess that he was about to light the tree. Wow, she had come at a good moment.

The man turned and threw a switch, and, indeed, the

lights on the giant upside-down tree came on, all beautiful blue and red.

But then something strange happened. A giant banner began to unroll from a horizontal pole set high above the platform. The crowd in the mezzanine gave an enormous cheer as more and more of the banner revealed itself. It showed a face, Rose saw.

It was a huge, forty-foot-high painting . . . of her.

Of Rose! It really was. It was black and white, and she wasn't smiling—she looked very sulky and serious, actually. But if there was any doubt, there was her name at the bottom, in huge italics: *ROSE*.

She could just make out the mayor saying something with a solemn expression on his face, and she could distinctly hear her name being intoned:

"Rose! Rose! Rose!"

The banner fluttered majestically in the air.

Rose wasn't just surprised. She was shocked. And a little frightened. A lot frightened, actually. It was the kind of thing she had always imagined happening in her daydreams—being celebrated in a strange and beautiful city—but now that it was happening, it was all too much. A slow pulse of panic grew in her stomach. It was the first time since walking to Central Park by herself that she remembered to be scared.

"Hey, o' course they're chantin' your name, Rosie-toes. They been waiting for you for a while. And hopin' for you for years!"

Rose turned. It was Ethan—well, Louis—looking very happy and prosperous, and not in overalls and a Peter Pan collar, but a three-piece checked suit and a peaked cap. Rose hugged him tight, she was so happy to see a familiar face. She trusted Louis for some reason, even if he had been an imposter.

"I knew you'd come, Rosie-toes. And you couldn't have arrived at a more, what's that word? Oh yes, *propitious*." He pronounced the big word carefully. "You couldn't have come to U Nork at a better moment."

Rose gulped. "How do they even know who I am?" she asked.

"Well, that's a long story, kiddo," Louis said. "I'll let Hizzoner himself explain it to ya. But we better get outta here first. We don't want people to see ya too soon, kiddo. We won't let the cat outta the bag that you're here, not for a while. Not *everybody* will be glad to see Rose here at last," he added darkly.

Rose felt frightened again; it seemed like there was an awful lot Louis wasn't telling her. But she reminded herself that all she had to do was have breakfast with the mayor, and the dog and a snow globe would be hers.

So Rose breathed in deep and ignored her fear.

"Ethan—I mean Louis—where am I?"

"Why, you're in the big town. You're in U Nork, just like you wanted."

"U Nork?"

"Yep, greatest city on earth—or under the earth, I guess I should say. I mean New York, where you live, is very nice. Very restful and serene and so on," he said, trying to be kind, "but it ain't U Nork." He gestured toward the enormous, busy city. "And this right here? This is Square Times Square Squared."

"Square Times Sq—what?" Rose asked, still hardly able to follow.

"Square Times Square *Squared*," Louis said patiently. "It was first named in honor of one of our politicians who ran on a platform of square times—you know, a fair deal for everyone. So we called it Square Times Square. But then they built it four times as big—you know, squared it. So it became Square Times Square Squared."

Rose tried to remember what she had learned about squaring things at school, but she couldn't really focus because Louis was more or less dragging her out of the beautiful square through the crowd, until they were back out on the busy street. They rushed by the great tower where Rose had almost been stuck on the elevator.

"Louis—" she began.

"You were wondering why they were taking their bags on the elevator? Call me psychic, kiddo! Actually, I was followin' you from the moment you arrived. See, people here in the big town take holidays on the upper floors, so they have to take the economy elevators. Eight hours going up! Not me, kiddo. Sheesh, if I can't go up in a first-class lift, I ain't going. I'll take the escalator for anything closer than the two hundred and second floor. Takes longer, sure, but it's more scenic. . . ."

He spat out a bit of his cigar.

"O' course, most of my travelin' is back and forth across the steps. The ones that cross the water. Just like you did, kid. That's the ticket! O' course, you gotta climb a ways, but then you can slide the banister all the way down. Next time, Rosie. Remember: every step you take goin' up is one glide down in the other direction. Take it down, kiddo. It's the wisdom of the streets. Street smarts."

Rose didn't know what to say, so she smiled politely.

"Speakin' of goin' up, you wanna see a really slick way to travel, Rosie-toes? Look there," he said, pointing behind her.

Rose turned to follow Louis's finger and saw a skein of fine lines in the sky, like a spiderweb, passing from one skyscraper to another. She squinted, peering even more carefully, and saw tiny figures scurrying across them.

"High-line walkers," said Louis casually. "Delivering packages from building to building could take weeks. All that business going down, across, and back up. So they just walk across the wires."

"But what happens if they fall?"

"Oh, they're not—well, look!"

And as Rose looked up, she could just make out one walker suddenly fret and lean over, looking very precarious. She gasped. He was falling!

Quick as a wink, one of the giant pigeons swooped underneath—and caught him! Just like the pigeons had done with the falling midgets the day before! She watched as the messenger put his arms around the giant pigeon's throat and swooped back to the wire.

"Well, that's good," Rose, said. "But why don't they just use the pigeons to fly from place to place?"

"They could. But it would cost a ton of money. It's three Norks a minute to ride a pigeon," he said. "You pay through the nose. . . . See—he's paying now."

Rose saw that the rescued messenger was indeed pulling coins from his right nostril and placing them in a basket on the pigeon's back.

So that's what paying through the nose looked like! She'd have to tell her dad.

"Hey, Rose!" Louis cried. "Enough gabbing! We got a

date!" And grasping her hand, he pulled her firmly down the boulevard behind him.

Rose looked around. It *was* a big town! Much bigger than New York. Why, Louis was right: it made New York look like the suburbs! The sidewalks were at least three times wider than they were back home—and not only were people skating, they were racing and running. Cars drove right onto the sidewalk. They blared their horns, and *whoosh*—they whisked across the sidewalk and up the side of the nearest building.

On the sidewalk, she noticed a number dispenser—the kind they have in bakeries—right at the edge of the street, where parking meters usually stood in New York. As people rushed past, Rose noticed that they all grabbed a paper slip with a number on it from the machine.

"Take a number! You gotta take a number before you get in line!" Louis called out to her.

Rose reached out, stabbing her hand in tentatively as all the other pedestrians grabbed at the dispenser. Finally she got her hand in and tore off a slip.

She looked at it. It was number 378797828.

"Louis," she asked, "am I the three hundred millionth . . . ah . . . three hundred seventy . . . seventy-eighth—oh, well, am I *that* far back in line?"

"Looks like it!" Louis said.

"Oh," Rose said, and thought for a moment. "What am I in line *for*?" she asked finally.

But Louis just shrugged. "It doesn't matter," he said. "But at least ya got your number! You always gotta take a number in U Nork."

But before Rose could even find out what kind of thing it was that she might have to take a number to wait for, to her horror, a person on the street was knocked sideways by one of the onrushing cars, and the car didn't even stop. Rose gasped. A second later, the pavement underneath the struck man revolved—turned right over—and he was gone.

Louis must have sensed Rose's terror. "Don't worry, kiddo!" he said. "He's in the basement infirmary. They'll have him as good as new. He'll lose a leg, maybe, but they can stick on a better one. If you went crying every time you got run over in U Nork," he said, "you'd be cryin' all day and night. Toughen up, kiddo. You're in the big town now. Anyway, there's not much life here on the side streets. Let's go on over to A-five."

"What's A-five?"

"It's like your Fifth Avenue."

"You have a Fifth Avenue, too?"

"We got everything you got," Louis explained. "Only better! Our Fifth Avenue used to be called that, back when the Flying Visitor first laid out the city plan. But it took too long to say. So we shortened it."

They turned the corner. This new street made the one they'd just left look like a small, narrow alley. It was a vast boulevard, lined with even higher towers, and *two* sidewalks, not one—the upper level elevated on pillars above the lower one—with people racing on skates and stilts and in dirigibles on both. There were even two sets of traffic lights, one for each level.

"Watch the droppings!" Louis cried. "Jeez, these new taxis! They got no decency in 'em, and no idea where to leave their, well, you know . . ."

Rose saw that there were great department stores on the streets, just as there were back in New York, with the same kind of huge windows filled with mannequins modeling clothes. But as she looked more closely she noticed that the mannequins in the windows, impeccably dressed, weren't made of plastic, but were actually moving and smiling and talking to each other. Were they robots? she wondered, as she drew closer.

"They're just your ordinary citizens," Louis said, as though reading her mind again. "Here in U Nork the government says you gotta do some mannequin duty, posing in windows for a week or so every few years. Just the way people do jury duty back in your town."

And Rose noticed that the living mannequins in the windows gravely winked at her as she passed, as though proud of doing their civic duty.

"Then who does the jury duty?" Rose asked.

"Oh, that. Well, that's done by—hey, kiddo, you hungry?"

Rose saw that, just like back in New York, there were food pushcarts lining the street. But these didn't just have hot dogs and falafel. FOIE GRAS ON A STICK, CAVIAR CRUMBS, STEAK AU POIVRE—FIFTY DOLLARS said the signs.

Louis saw her look at the pushcarts. "Ya hungry, kid?" he repeated.

She shook her head since she didn't want to ruin her appetite if she was supposed to have breakfast with the mayor, but it was already well past breakfast time, and her stomach grumbled loudly in opposition.

Louis smiled. "Don't blame ya. Bit peckish myself. We've got time for a quick lunch, I guess, and I'm sure the mayeh won't mind just having tea with ya. Why don't we go to the French place? Ya like Norkian food?" And without waiting for her to speak, he elbowed his way right past the crowd—knocking down three women and their children, who all landed splat on the pavement with their packages.

"Louis! Shouldn't we watch where we're going?" Rose said.

Louis shrugged as they reached the edge of the

pavement. "That's alright where *you* come from, where everybody's got all day to do everything. Around here, if you can't stand the elbows, keep offa the sidewalk." He chuckled to himself at his own joke.

When they got to the pushcart, Rose was startled to see a maître d' standing in front of it.

He smiled obsequiously at Louis. "How many, Monsieur Louis?" The crowds kept jostling them from behind, but Louis didn't seem to notice.

"Two! We're in the mood for a little leisurely lunch."

Rose was glad that they had time to eat. She enjoyed good food. Then she looked up.

A human pyramid loomed over her—five layers of people perched on stools that stretched three stories high in the air, with a long spiral bar swooping down toward the pavement. The only way up, she thought, must be to climb onto the shoulders of the other diners.

"Right this way, monsieur!" the maître d' said, pointing to two tiny stools on the top level. "The best seats in the house. Follow me."

"They know me here," Louis whispered to Rose with a wink. And just like her father might, he took her hand and pulled her toward two stools that were perched precariously high on the pyramid of eaters. He hoisted her onto the shoulders of a hatted man, who was himself sitting on the shoulders of the diners lower down.

Rose rocked uneasily, trying to keep her balance on this stranger's shoulders. But he seemed to ignore her and went right on eating his soup and reading his paper. Rose, Louis, and the maître d' continued to climb, clutching people's cuffs and hauling themselves up to stand on their shoulders, moving up the pyramid of diners as casually as if they were steps to a restaurant. When they finally got to the top, the maître d' dusted off the two stools and very grandly pointed to them. Rose slipped in right beside her neighbor.

She looked down, then quickly looked back up. It was so precarious! She expected to see the maître d' climb back down over the bodies of his diners, but instead he leaped right off, folding his napkin over his head into a graceful bow, like a parachute, and floating gently back down to his station.

"I love to eat with a view of the kitchen," Louis said, half to himself. He was looking across the street. Rose looked there, too.

Was that the kitchen?

She tried to steady herself on her stool and really look at her surroundings. The kitchen was all the way across the street. A squadron of men in white aprons and hats was gathered, the traffic roaring between them and the human pyramid of diners. But they didn't have copper pots and pans like ordinary chefs. Instead they looked like soldiers, lined up in rows and armed with small cannons and catapults.

"What'll it be, Rosie?" Louis asked.

But before she could say a word, Louis looked at the waiter and said, "We'll start with the onion soup, salad, filet of beef with sauce béarnaise, tarte tatin, a double cap, and bring the check, please."

The waiter nodded.

Within half a second, there were soup plates in front of them. Rose had barely lifted her spoon when she saw Louis had already picked up his bowl and drank his right down. How rude! Rose thought, as she turned back to her own bowl. But before her spoon had even touched her soup, the waiter whisked the bowl away. He quickly dumped the uneaten soup into a silver flask he'd taken from the sash on his waist.

Then, to her surprise, the waiter spun her empty bowl across the street, above the roaring traffic, right past the nose of an onrushing pigeon on its way to earth, where it was caught by a dishwasher standing on the other side of the street, who washed it, dried it, and, with a flick of his wrist, sent it spinning back, clean and dry, right toward where they sat. People ducked casually as the spinning Frisbee-like plate passed over their heads. One man lost a hat. Then he cursed and picked it up.

"Louis," Rose began to say. "Why—"

But before she could finish her question, Louis had looked across the street and opened his mouth wide, signaling to Rose to do the same.

From across the street the cooks began firing bits of steak from their cannon and French fried potatoes from their catapults directly into Louis's wide-open mouth. One of the cooks held a hose and very skillfully fired a yellowy liquid that Rose thought must be the béarnaise sauce directly into Louis's mouth along with the steak.

Rose was so busy watching Louis eating that she forgot she'd ordered the same meal. She suddenly felt a pelting of hot food on the side of her head. Then she made the mistake of turning toward the kitchen and—*splat*, the steak and potatoes fired directly into her face. She ducked down quickly to avoid the thundering stream of sauce. Luckily, it passed right over her head.

"Good reflexes, kid," Louis said, shutting his mouth briefly between "bites."

Rose tentatively lifted her head, being careful to keep her mouth wide open this time. As she did, a stream of food fired from across the street landed in her mouth. It was a gentler sensation than she had imagined it would be.

The chefs had very good aim. Rose clamped down to chew, and signaled with her hand that she had had enough. It was too scary having your food sort of *shot* at you.

"I love this place," Louis said, looking around after his meal was finished, which took about twenty seconds. "Look! You got people having a business lunch . . ."

He pointed with his chin toward two men a couple of levels down the shaky human pyramid. They were chewing food while the waiters fired condiments and garnishes directly into their mouths. At the same time, the businessmen's fingers worked the keyboards of each other's open computers.

"And then you've got what you might call your romantic rendezvous," Louis added, looking across the pyramid of diners and shaking his head ruefully as though remembering something.

Rose followed his gaze. Just one row up, a man and woman were locked in an embrace, their heads resting on each other's shoulders, while two waiters stood on either side of them and shot chocolates and smoked salmon and a stream of champagne into their mouths from either side. A third waiter rapidly played a violin.

"Yeah. *Real* romantic. I brought Doris here on our first Valentine's Day date. Wined and dined her with chocolates and filet mignon. What a night! Must have taken ten minutes, that meal. Boy, was I in love. But like I always tell Doris, you only marry your first wife once!" He chuckled at his own joke. Rose thought it was more strange than romantic. Like fish being fed . . .

"Okay, kiddo, enough lying around. You want some coffee?" Louis asked next. "Oh, I forgot, you're a kid. Me, if it weren't for caffeine, I don't know what I'd do. Yeah, coffee!" he said to the waiter, who had suddenly reappeared. "Forget the double cap! Give me a bush!"

Rose watched the cooks across the street set an entire coffee tree on fire before picking up the hoses. While one chef shot the roasted coffee beans through the air into Louis's mouth, another sprayed hot water and steamed milk. The two flows intersected, and within five seconds—it couldn't have been more—Louis had drunk an entire tree's worth of coffee, latte style.

"Now, that gives you a little lift, don't it?" he said.

Moments later, a small paper airplane flew right across the street and landed in Louis's lap.

Louis unfolded it and gave it a quick scan. Rose realized it must be the check and started to reach into her coat pocket to see if she had any money. But Louis waved her off with a quick turn of his wrist, then took the check and bit down on it hard.

"They got my tooth marks on record, o' course," he

explained. "That's the way you charge a bill here. Just bite down on the bill. . . . You either gotta pay through the nose or pay through your teeth," he concluded gaily, and grabbing Rose, who so far had eaten one bite of steak, he parachuted the two of them back down to the pavement and into the rushing crowds. Clean and dirty plates whizzed by their heads, and Rose ducked while men with the latte hoses continued spraying strong coffee into the waiting mouths of customers.

Rose checked her watch. It was 2:22. They had spent exactly one and a half minutes having a three-course lunch.

"That was Rocco's," Louis said, suppressing a little belch. "Nice spot. But it's just too slow to survive in this day and age. Who's got that kind of time for lunch anymore? Anyway, you got a date with the mayeh—and that means we gotta run."

But they couldn't have run if they tried. The press of people on the brightly lit street was even fiercer than it had been when she'd arrived. People raced by at blazing speeds, and paperboys were shouting, "Hyper-extra!" She noticed that a few of the businessmen on wheelies had small, battery powered motors attached, to make them go even faster.

"It's a shame, you hadda arrive in U Nork right in the middle of the night this way." Louis shook his head.

"Burg's practically dead. Wait till you get here at the height of rush hour . . . Whoa, baby . . ."

Rose looked at him. He seemed serious.

"'Dead'? 'Middle of the night'? Louis," she said, "I thought we just had *lunch*."

"It was," Louis insisted. "We have lunch all day in our town, the way they have breakfast all day in your town. But the night's got what you might call poetry . . ."

Rose looked around again. "Louis—how can it be the middle of the night? The sun's out and—"

"Oh, that ain't the *sun*, sweetheart, it's—" Louis looked at his watch. "Well, it should be going on nighttime light any minute now. Depends on who buys the star rights and moon namings, see."

And to her shock, the sun started to dim. Not set; it didn't fall slowly to the horizon, as it did at home. No, right there in the height of the sky, the bright white sun began to dim, growing duller and fainter, as if someone had turned a dimmer switch. No one on the street seemed to notice.

Stars began to appear in the sky. They seemed to glimmer, like jewels, as though they were made of many colors, not just bright star white. Rose looked closer and saw that the colors glimmering within the stars were really writing, as if someone had written a message in the stars.

Bop'n'Glo
STAR SNAX
Blammo!
Drink Kodo-Kola!
CHEW CHOC-O
ZUG MEANS Z-Z-Z
Whammo!
EAT MORE NOW!

She squinted and tried to make it out. "Nesso." Yes, that was it. "Nesso: For Full Bold Coffee Flavor."

"It's a commercial," she said, disappointed.

"Well o' course. We've been selling the sky for a long time. Just the way ya sell them dinky little signs back in your town."

The stars in the night sky were much bigger than the stars back home, and she saw now that every star in the sky was lit up with a slogan, or a picture, or something zooming up or down. Smoke came out of some of the stars, advertising tea, while other stars had faces on them, smiling and gleaming until she saw nothing but bright white teeth in bright pink lips. Then the mouth itself disappeared and she saw in lettering, high in the night sky: DENTITO: FOR THAT BRIGHT NORKIAN GLEAM. And near it was another blinking star with the words STAR SNAX.

Even the moon, if that's what it was, showed a woman who kept winking and feeding more pie to the smiling man on the star nearest her.

"Is it really, you know, appropriate, to sell the sky?"

"We're a town built on money, ya could say, Rosie-toes. A fact no one knows better than the mayeh. Come on or you'll be late. He'll tell you everything you need to know."

"And if I go, he'll give me a dog?" Rose reminded him.

She hated to seem greedy, but it was easy to think that Louis might forget about it if she wasn't persistent.

"Oh, you'll get a dog," he said. "Don't worry. Ya got a pocket don't ya?"

Rose reached down, puzzled. She certainly had a pocket. But she didn't know what that had to do with anything.

By the time she looked up, a good thirty people had already separated the two of them; he had raced ahead of her on the grand avenue.

"And what about the snow globe?" she called after him.

Louis didn't turn around. "Oh, you'll get that, too!" he cried, lifting his hands above his head, as though signaling the sky in his excitement.

She ran after him, puzzled but happy, dodging and weaving as she followed him through the crowded moonlit boulevards.

Chapter Four

WITH THE MAYOR

Louis raced along the wide street, Rose following close behind. The press of people bumping into her and racing past her, their heads high and completely indifferent to her presence—which at first had been so weird and frightening— now felt familiar. Walking on these streets was like wading in the ocean, she thought: you just watched for the waves, and tried not to let the pebbles on the ocean floor strike your shins.

Ahead of her, Louis seemed like a rabbit running through a maze, leaping and bounding through the teeming crowd. Suddenly, he stopped.

"This is takin' too long," he said. "You only got so much time here. We better grab a pigeon." Peering into the sky, Louis put two fingers in his mouth and let out a piercing whistle. Nothing. Then suddenly, a huge pigeon appeared, fluttering its wings before them. It settled in the street, nearly squashing four or five indignant pedestrians, who shook their fists at the big gray bird. Taking Rose by the hand, Louis forced his way to the curb and jumped aboard the pigeon, hoisting Rose up after him.

"City Hall," he said, "and step on it."

The pigeon glanced back at them with a bored, hooded look.

"There's traffic there up the kazoo. You want me to take the Cloud-Way?" the pigeon asked.

"And charge me ten shekels extra!" Louis nearly shrieked. "No. Take the usual."

The pigeon shrugged (and if you've never seen a pigeon shrug, it's very impressive—kind of lofty and indifferent).

"Okay, pal, suit yourself. But don't blame me if we're stuck in traffic for the next twenty minutes. Hey! Where you going there? What the heck you think you're doing there? Go back and buy a canary!" the pigeon shouted. These last words were addressed to another pigeon that was trying to occupy the same air space. This pigeon shot them a dirty look, but then they were aloft.

Rose was certainly startled to discover that the pigeons in this city were not only big, but that they worked for a living and complained a lot.

"Hey, quit flapping your jaw and start flapping your wings!" Louis said. It was a bit surprising how rude everyone was in U Nork, but Rose supposed that was just because they had to live right on top of one another.

Up and up they went! Rose's stomach turned over the way it had that summer when she and Oliver had gone on the upper ramp of a roller coaster. She clutched Louis around the waist, frightened of falling off, and shut her eyes. Her stomach rolled again—they were so high up. But holding Louis tight, she opened one eye and looked down with fascination.

They were high above the city. Rose could see everything passing below them. She was reminded of the view from the Empire State Building; everything looked flat and funny so high up. But here in U Nork the sky itself was full of objects. Down below, snaking in and out of the skyscrapers, was what looked like an enormous roller coaster, swooping and rising and falling and turning throughout the city's streets; the cars along it looked like subway cars, with bright headlights mounted on the lead car beaming through the darkness.

"That's the supway," Louis said, as though reading her mind. "We call it that because you can eat on it if you're in a hurry. Have supper and get where you're going. We couldn't put it underground like your subway because—"

But he suddenly stopped speaking, as though he had said something he shouldn't have.

It was true night now, and everything was illuminated. In soft starlight they flew directly around the shining turrets and gleaming fins of the U Nork skyscrapers. They flew past and circled right around the zeppelins and balloons, which trailed long advertising signs: NESSO COFFEE or BUY MALARKEY NAIL POLISH. MAKES YOUR FELLA SIGH.

The cool night wind breezed past them as their pigeon taxi plunged through the night. Rose looked up at the sky. It looked more opaque than the sky looked back home, like shimmering black velvet fabric cut up by star points.

"Louis, why are the pigeons here so big?" Rose asked sleepily as their bird swooped and thrust through the dark sky.

"It's simple. We raise the baby pigeons in your city, until they're big enough to cross the steps—then we train 'em here to take passengers. That way you get the mess of the untrained pigeons, and we have a place to keep 'em safe."

Safe from what? Rose wondered. But she was too fascinated by everything around her to ask.

At last the pigeon settled down on one of the most elaborate of all the many towering buildings. The tower rose right up into the clouds. There were little statues on its spires, busts of men and women looking snootily toward the sky. Their names were inscribed in stone below and Rose noticed how odd they were: a man named Fisher next to one of a woman named Fibeudil. There was also a very proud-looking young boy named Upstart next to a man named Downwind.

"Those are all the ex-mayors of U Nork," Louis said proudly. "It's a lottery job. You never know who's going to get it. . . ."

Rose looked up and saw, above the columns and the pediment, a simple motto chiseled into the marble: RETURNUS NOBIS SHALLUS.

"What does that mean, Louis?" she asked.

"We shall return."

Rose looked at him, puzzled.

"The mayeh will explain! Or rather, the second permanent assistant sub-mayor will," Louis said.

A guard of honor emerged from the penthouse of City Hall and, bowing deeply, escorted them into the lobby, where, very ceremoniously, they all waited for an elevator.

Within minutes, an elevator whisked them toward the council room of City Hall. They came out in a broad corridor lined with red carpets, where uniformed men with braided trousers saluted Rose as she walked by. Even Louis, normally so brash and self-confident, seemed a little subdued.

At the end of the corridor, two figures were waiting for them. There was a boy, not much older than Rose herself, with a big chain around his neck, and beside him, a beaming older man, who looked a bit like Santa Claus after a hot shave.

"Greetings, Rose," the boy said carefully, reading a prepared text. "Long have the people of U Nork awaited you. I, the mayor of this fine city, make you, with this ring . . . Where's the ring?" He put the paper aside while he searched for it. "Oh, here it is. Well, with this ring, we make you a full citizen of the serene republic, the city of U Nork."

Rose wasn't sure what to do at such an awkward, formal moment, so she curtsied deeply, the way she had been taught to do when she'd had a very small role in *The Nutcracker* the previous winter. Then she accepted the ring and put it on her finger.

"Very good, Miss Rose. Very good, your worship the mayor," said the little beaming man beside the boy. It startled Rose to see a grown man being so deferential to a small boy. "Still, time is short—as short as the mayor is, one might say." He paused as though expecting a laugh. When he didn't get one, he went on. "I am the second permanent assistant sub-mayor, on permanent staff here at City Hall."

"You see, the mayor is just whoever wins the lottery, but the second permanent assistant sub-mayor stays on staff," Louis, at her elbow, explained. "We call him the SPASM. Like a whudyacallit, an anagram? S.P.A.S.M."

"You mean an acronym, I think," Rose said politely.

"Everyone calls him the Spaz, for short," the young mayor whispered under his breath.

Rose saw the SPASM shoot him a look.

"What happened to the first permanent assistant sub-mayor?" Rose asked.

There was silence.

"A predictably penetrating question from a predictably penetrating mind," the SPASM said, impressed. "What happened is—well, the whole thing takes some explaining. Perhaps Your Honor would like to invite Citizen Rose into the Control Room?"

The mayor-boy stared at him dumbly before finally getting the hint. "Oh! Yeah! Right this way."

It was a weird arrangement, Rose thought. Obviously the mayor had the official power, but the SPASM had all the smarts.

"Yeah, it is a weird arrangement," Louis said, once again reading her mind. "But see, if the SPASM had all the power and know-how, it would be dangerous for the city. This way, a different guy has the power every year, and the same guy has the know-how all the time, so it works out. People with power should be dumb, and the people around them smart. Like in school. That's the U Nork way!"

They followed the mayor and the SPASM through a giant door and into a giant domed space, twice as high as the school auditorium.

The place took Rose's breath away. It was sort of like pictures she had seen of Mission Control in Houston, where the space shots came from. There were television screens up and down the walls, monitored by people in short-sleeved white shirts. But instead of being high-tech and made of steel and glass, the room was paneled in mahogany and rose-colored wood, with the television screens set deep within the wood. A soft murmur of noise blanketed the room.

Rose approached the television screens and blinked with surprise. They were all showing scenes of New York City, her home! One was of the view outside Bloomingdale's, others showed the inside of the subway; some surveyed the park, and a couple monitored schoolrooms like her own. And many of them—she was sure of it—showed the insides of gyms, just like the one she had passed with her family in the taxi only two nights before. Middle-aged people were pedaling hard and sweating desperately on their stationary bikes and panting on their treadmills. She looked up at the sign above those screens: CAUTION! POWER STATION! it read.

Rose looked inquisitively at the SPASM. He smiled. "Yes, you see, that's how we get enough power to run our city. From all the exercise people do in *your* city. You supply it," the SPASM announced triumphantly, gesturing toward the video images of the sweating gym-goers. "That's why we planted all those bikes and treadmills and workout rooms in the last thirty years. Show her!" he ordered.

Suddenly all the many television screens were alight with the same image: sweaty men and women in New York, working desperately hard, panting and perspiring in their tracksuits.

"We run cables and lines from all those machines," the SPASM went on.

The screens were showing, in cartoon animation, how the turning wheels and belts of New Yorkers exercising on their gym machines electrified cables that went deep into the earth, turning flywheels and generators at the earth's core.

"Then they feed directly into our power generators here," he continued, and Rose saw in the animation all of the electrical wires leading right into the center of U Nork itself, to a huge generating station with four chimneys. "So all that exercise in New York gives us power here in U Nork!" the SPASM concluded. "The harder your parents work out, the more energy there is for our city. It's a very good arrangement!"

"Why do you watch us so closely?" Rose asked.

"Because our two cities are linked. Small and poky, backward and old-fashioned as your city may be, Rose, it still matters to us." He smiled very sincerely. "You live up there on top of the earth," he gestured toward the ceiling, "and we long ago took refuge down here, underneath. But it was seeing your city that inspired us to build our city, even if our city is far finer than yours."

"You see, Rose, everything in New York explains everything in U Nork—and everything in U Nork explains everything in New York. We first got the idea to build our city to be like your city when the Flying Visitor came to Old Nork in his gray zeppelin, a long time ago. He played us records, and taught us dialect—that's how I learned to speak all elegant like this!" Louis added very gravely, as though Rose should be impressed by the way he spoke. She nodded.

"And he also showed us pictures and photos and plans of New York. We were all so impressed, we decided to rebuild our city to look like yours. It was just such a great town! So we asked the Visitor to lay it out for us, the grid and the numbered streets and the avenues. Grand Central Terminal! The park right in the middle! We asked him to copy it all!"

"Of course, we asked for some, well, improvements," the SPASM continued. "We saw from the pictures your city wasn't really entirely up to snuff. I mean—such short and tiny buildings! Such bare and empty streets! So we built higher and higher and made Old Nork bigger and better."

Rose's head was spinning.

"And when we moved, we just took everything along with us. So here we are, in U Nork, the biggest and grandest city in the solar system!"

"Move? Why'd you have to move?" Rose asked.

"Ah. I knew you were going to ask that." The SPASM snapped his fingers. Suddenly, all the television monitors filled with color, and, instead of showing scenes from New York, they showed what looked like old hand-painted images of some other city, far away. Orchestral music filled the big room.

"Long ago, Rose," the SPASM went on, "planet Nork was at the very edge of the solar system. It was hidden from observation by being tucked cunningly behind the other planets."

Now all the screens were showing pictures, sort of like a travelogue, of old days on the planet Nork. It looked like a great place to live, Rose thought. There were nice villages, and everyone wore togas.

"Hot!" Louis said.

"Nork was a beautiful planet. A pleasure spot full of life and variety, with an average yearly temperature of ninety degrees. And it had very light gravity, so it was easy to build as high as we wanted to. A hundred stories! Two hundred stories! Three hundred stories!"

"And so on . . ." Louis quickly added. Rose could tell that if he didn't interfere, the SPASM might just go enumerating the heights of skyscrapers.

The SPASM gave Louis a baleful look. But then he stopped.

"Alas—we built too high, and we became too proud of the beauty of our city, and at last the eyes of the Ice Queen were drawn to Nork."

"The Ice Queen!" Rose said, quite interested.

"Many stories have been written about her, many books, and even many strange sad songs," the SPASM said. "Others know her as Persephone, Queen of the Winter. She is a queen, and a goddess, and long ago a splinter of ice entered her eye, and turned her heart cold and greedy. All she wants are clean, cold things: ice, and snow, and diamonds. All she cares for is owning and keeping . . . and she wanted to own the planet of Nork. . . ."

Now the whole room darkened. The skyline of Old Nork appeared on the screens, with its tall towers lit up. And then, out of nowhere, two enormous dark eyes, like cat's eyes, narrow, hooded, and slanted, appeared on the horizon—dim at first, but growing brighter and brighter until their radiance erased all the other illumination in the sky. Nothing but two great eyes, vast as galaxies, stared down at the city. The music growled and grew as ominous as the sight. And Rose heard a woman's voice cry out, shrilly but sadly: "I shall put ice in the parks, and crush each tower with the weight of a hundred winters' snows in one night! Nork will be mine!"

Rose reflexively threw her hands up to cover her eyes. She peeked through a V-shaped slit between her pointer and middle finger.

"Impressive, eh? We made the presentation specially for ya," Louis said. He lifted himself to his tiptoes. "It's okay, Rose," he whispered in her ear.

"We knew our planet was always in her mind, and that she dreamed of bringing a new Ice Age to Nork. We were frightened that we couldn't defeat her. So we had to flee!" the SPASM said.

Now the music turned into a minor key, played with a cello, and Rose saw the people of Nork boarding old-fashioned-looking spaceships, clutching their children in bundles as they abandoned their planet.

"We packed our city and our citizens up and wandered the stars for years with our people asleep in suspended animation and only a few leaders still awake, searching for a new home. And at last we found one, safe and deep, beneath the welcoming planet Earth. We set out to build a new city on this planet—a secret city, away from the prying, spying eyes of the Ice Queen, who still vowed to pursue and destroy us. For decades now, we have been safe, deep and buried here, in our vast and beautiful city of U Nork."

"That means *New* Nork, really," Louis explained. "*U* is the prefix in Norkian that means 'new.'"

"But why Nork? What have you got that means so much to her? It can't just be your tall buildings," Rose said, her heart pounding in her chest so loudly she was sure Louis and the others could hear it.

Louis looked uncomfortably at the mayor, and the mayor looked at Louis, and Louis looked at the SPASM, and they all had those "Shall we tell her, or shall we not?" looks that people have when there's scary or sad or upsetting news.

"We've invited her all this way," Louis said. "It's too late to back out now."

The city officials nodded.

"Steam up the elevator," Louis said, rubbing his hands together. "We're goin' *down!*"

A few moments later, Rose found herself on the City Hall elevator with Louis, the SPASM, and the mayor.

Down and down the elevator went! Past the thousandth floor, then below the eight hundreds, down and down. Rose followed the floors on the lights above the doors.

Now they were at the "L" for Lobby. But still the elevator went down: Basement, Sub-Basement, Sub-Sub-Basement . . . until finally it arrived at a floor that lit up the very bottom of the panel. SUB-SUB-SUB-SUB-SUB-SUB-SUB-SUB-SUB BASEMENT, it read.

The car stopped. Rose swallowed to clear her ears.

"We're here," Louis said. "The Showroom."

The elevator doors opened. A dark corridor lay in front of them. Rose took a tentative step outside. A single beam of intense white light divided the hall.

Then she saw that the light came from below, from a crack in the floor itself. Two Norkian soldiers stood guard. They came to life as they saw Louis, the SPASM, and particularly Rose.

The SPASM held Rose back.

"Open the gates," he said to the guards grimly. "Let her see the foundation."

Rose heard gears crank and wheels turn. Slowly the floor slid apart. There was a dazzling, blinding white light—no, not white. Multicolored, as varied and bright as all the facets of a diamond.

She knelt down. That's what it was! A diamond, vast as

an underground cavern. A diamond at the very core of the earth!

"The biggest diamond in the universe," the SPASM whispered. His face was lit eerily from below by the giant gem. "And it's the foundation of our city. It's what U Nork is built on."

Rose saw that a fine mist of diamond dust rose from the diamond. She held out her hand. The diamond dust settled in it.

"I told ya U Nork was built on money," Louis said to Rose.

"It's . . . beautiful!" Rose said, struggling to find a word that captured exactly how ravishing it was.

"The Ice Queen thinks so too," the SPASM said. "You see, Rose, the Ice Queen wants nothing more than to steal the diamond from us."

"She's the one who's been following you!" Louis added. "The woman with the cat eyes."

"Forgive me for asking, but . . . why not just, well, give it to her, if she wants it so much?" Rose asked, shielding her eyes from the beautiful bright light.

"Why?" the SPASM almost cried. "Because it's the foundation of our city! It's our bedrock. We can't give her the diamond any more than the people in your city could give her the ground and the river. Give her the diamond, and all of U Nork—the towers, the squares, and the supway—it

would all crash to the ground! We are our diamond. And our diamond is our city."

"See, Rosie, in our original solar system, on Nork, our sun had got all compressed—" Louis began.

"Oh, I know about this!" Rose said. "The sun gets compressed and turns into a diamond!"

"Yeah, well what they *didn't* tell you is that the planets that go around that sun, well, naturally they're made of diamonds too. Planets come spinning off the sun and then when they cool, they're made of whatever the sun is made of—a diamond sun means diamond planets! So if the Ice Queen stole our diamond, she'd completely destroy U Nork in the process."

"But we were all safe here, hidden beneath the earth, our diamond tucked away—until just two months ago. She's—well, now she's spotted us!" the SPASM said. "Somehow she knows we are here. We have seen the eyes—the eyes above the city. And we knew that once she found us it would not be long before she came to destroy us again."

"And only you, Rosie-toes, can stop her!" Louis exclaimed.

"Me?" Rose said.

"Yes! After her eyes first appeared in the sky a few days ago, a small sign ya might say arose . . ." Louis said.

"We saw your beaming and gracious face in the sky!"

the SPASM continued. "What an apparition! And we heard your name whispering through the sky above our city: 'Rose!' So, we sent word to all of the brave and observant midgets working on the other side of the steps to find you. And Louis, our agent at your fine progressive school, came through! He called you here to our rescue." The SPASM was becoming extremely emotional.

"You gotta save us," Louis's rough voice cut through.

This whole thing was beginning to take on the shape of a massive misunderstanding, Rose thought to herself.

But before she could speak, Louis said, "Nobody's face appears in the sky without a reason. *Somebody* wants you to rescue us. We got no place left to go, baby. You gotta find a way to save U Nork."

"But I'm—"

Rose didn't know what to say. A great city hidden from the whole solar system, people in exile, hers to save—it was all too much to deal with.

"I wouldn't even know where to begin!" Rose said.

Louis and the SPASM looked at each other with a bit of bewilderment.

"Well, ma'am, we rather thought that you'd just sort of—*know*," the SPASM said at last.

But Rose merely shook her head.

A heavy silence filled the room.

Rose felt very bad. She felt that she had let them all down . . . but it's hard not to let people down when you don't know yourself exactly what's up. And that was the case here: she had loved her time in U Nork, and its history was certainly interesting, but what it all had to do with *her*, she could hardly imagine. She thought she ought to at least say something encouraging, though.

So she said, simply, "Louis, I'll do everything I can when I get back to New York to find out, well, everything I can—and if I can find any way to be helpful to you and save the city, I promise that I will."

"Thanks, kid," the SPASM said. "I guess that's all you can do."

Suddenly, Louis looked at his pocket watch.

"Oh, darn. We've been talking too long! You're going to have to go home! Get back here soon, Rose. Use the bridge. I guess you'd better go now. It's getting late."

Rose nodded and buttoned her coat. Both Louis and the SPASM looked so sad that Rose felt almost bad about mentioning the next thing, but—

"What about my dog?" she asked, politely but firmly.

The SPASM looked at Louis, and then Louis at the SPASM.

"I did promise her a dog."

"Well, you'd better show her the kennels, then," the SPASM said tersely.

Rose's ears pricked up. The kennels of U Nork! This would be fun. They would probably have to take another elevator, and there would be puppies barking and jumping everywhere.

Instead, Louis simply reached into his inner pocket, and, after first drawing out a couple of old cigar butts and his pocket watch, he finally found a little plush box, about the size of a paperback book.

"Listen!" he said to Rose, holding the plush box out to her.

Rose pressed her ear against the box, but she couldn't hear a thing.

"I guess they're all asleep," said Louis tenderly. "Sweet little things!"

The SPASM opened the box. Rose looked inside.

In tiny velvet-lined compartments, there were dogs. They were not just tinier than any dogs Rose had ever seen, but tinier than she had ever imagined dogs could be. The biggest ones were no bigger than her thumb, and the smallest ones were barely the size of her fingernail.

"You said you wanted a little dog, right?" said Louis. "Well, why don't you take one."

They looked so small and fragile, Rose was almost afraid to touch them, but at last she reached in and, very gingerly, extracted one tiny puppy from the velvet box, holding it on the very tip of her finger. What kind of a dog was this?

Did she really *want* a dog like this?

She squinted hard, and could see him looking up at her. He opened his minuscule mouth and seemed to howl. She lowered her head to listen, and could just hear, as though it were coming from miles away, a clear, infinitesimal bark.

"See, Rose?" Louis said. "You get the baby pigeons, and we get the baby dogs. When they get big and messy, we send them back to New York, for you to deal with."

"I'll call him Spot," she said, "because he's no bigger than a spot. And I'll love him with all my heart." And Rose put Spot carefully into the pocket of her violet coat. She thought he would be safe there. She could just barely feel him wriggle and explore inside.

And before she could say thank you, Rose, with a shudder and a start, felt herself lying in the dark on something hard and damp. She rolled over and opened her eyes. Everything was dim and gray, but she could see that she was back on the grass in Central Park, near the pond, where she had started. She looked up in the sky. It looked like the early morning—like dawn! She turned and saw a single police car turning around as it patrolled the park. She'd better get back home before they saw her!

Rose picked herself up, dusted off her beautiful violet coat, and hurried home.

Chapter Five

LUNCH WITH JOE MURPHY

Had she been dreaming? U Nork certainly felt like a dream. The towers, the long ride on the back of the passenger pigeon, the advertisements in the night sky . . . just like a dream. Had she just fallen asleep on the lawn of Central Park and somehow slept through the night?

Rose walked the ten blocks home and sneaked into the apartment with her mother's key, which she carefully put back in the kitchen before going to her room.

And then she remembered Spot. She reached into her pocket and searched for him with a single finger. Nothing.

Had he been a dream, too?

Then she felt the tiniest vibration. She drew out her finger.

There he was! Spot! The fingernail-size puppy with a

wet nose. So it hadn't been a dream! It was all real, and completely strange.

Spot licked her finger and whimpered gently. Rose figured he was hungry and decided to go into the kitchen and look for something for him to eat. It was a good thing that she had remembered to put her nightgown on over her jeans, because her father was already there having breakfast.

"Hey, Partly," he said warmly as he ate buttered toast. "Aren't you late for school?"

"No school today, Dad. It's a professional day for the teachers."

Her father sighed. "Professional day. They count their money and then write me a letter asking for more. That's their profession."

Rose didn't respond. She cast a nervous eye around the kitchen. Spot was shifting in her pocket. He could probably smell the food. Was there anything there that Spot could eat? What *would* a tiny Norkian dog eat? She looked at the counter and noticed there were crumbs all along it. That might work. She cautiously walked over and swept some of them into her hand.

"Hey, Partly, why do you have your clothes on under your nightgown?" he asked.

Rose gulped. "Oh, I was cold," she said at last.

Her father seemed to accept it. Grown-ups in New

York, Rose had noticed, usually accepted stupid explanations. Without looking up from his paper, he said, "Well, if you've got school off today, kid, what's your plan? All-day homework session?"

More like research, she thought to herself—about U Nork and the Ice Queen and celestial travel. It was the least she could do for the people who gave her Spot. But she didn't even know where to begin.

Suddenly a thought occurred to her.

The SPASM had said, "Everything in New York explains everything in U Nork. And everything in U Nork explains everything in New York," right? Well, thinking it over, she realized it implied that the trick to finding out something about U Nork might be learning more about New York. So who better to ask than Mr. Murphy, the oldest living writer at the magazine where her father worked as a cartoonist? Mr. Murphy knew everything about anything to do with New York, so he might very well know something about U Nork—or at least where to look!

"Dad. Since I have the day off from school, could I come to the office with you and—and maybe have lunch with you and Mr. Murphy?" she asked, trying to sound casual and shrugging her shoulders.

"You want to have lunch with old Joe?" her father said. "You two have a nice friendship. You're probably the only one who does, Rose," her father added. "Sure. I'll be leaving in about half an hour."

Rose sneaked back into her room and took Spot out of her pocket. There he was, tiny and eager as ever. She took the crumbs from her palm, and held one out tentatively to him. He leaped up in the air, a tiny leap, but a real one, and licked the crumb from her finger. She could feel his small, cool wet tongue against her flesh. A thrill of excitement, and even a kind of love, swept through her. Okay, he was a *small* dog. But he was still hers.

But after tasting the crumb carefully with his tongue, Spot flicked it out and drew back on his hind legs and made the tiniest of disgruntled snarls. It sounded like a distant whistle.

Oh, dear, Rose thought. Her heart beat faster. She had forgotten to ask what Norkian dogs eat.

She walked over to Oliver's door and knocked. "Oliver?" she called. She wanted to borrow her brother's computer to do an online search about tiny Norkian dogs. The FAQ would probably include a frequently asked question about what they liked to eat. And, it would give her a chance to show Spot to Oliver, which she wanted to do more than anything.

"Yeah? It's open," he answered absently.

Cupping Spot in her palm, she went into Oliver's room.

She was ready to take out her Norkian dog and amaze him, but he was sitting on the floor, surrounded by his magic books and staring at a video.

"Come here. Let me try the watch steal on you again!"

Rose sighed, slipped Spot into her pocket—the big reveal could wait two minutes, she figured—and walked over to her brother. She held out her wrists, and then pretended not to notice when he pumped her arms and slipped off her watch.

"Didja notice that?" he asked anxiously.

"Well, of course I *noticed* it," Rose said. "I mean, you told me you were going to steal my watch. . . ."

"Oh, rats," Oliver said. "You're not supposed to notice it."

"Well, somebody who wasn't warned wouldn't have noticed it," Rose said, wanting to encourage him. "You did it very well."

But he just frowned at her, shook his head, and went back to reading his magic books.

Rose waited for a minute, and then said, as tactfully as she could: "Oliver, can I please do a search on your computer?"

"Not now. Come back later," he said.

"But, Oliver—"

"But what? I'm a little busy now," he said, holding up a handful of cards.

Rose slunk out back through the hallway and into her bedroom.

At least Mr. Murphy was an extremely good listener, Rose thought. She jumped on her bed and took out Spot. Stroking him gently between the ears, she thought about how Mr. Murphy would put his head to one side, squint seriously, and then sort of coo sympathetically with her story, saying, "I know," only it took half a minute to say and sounded like: "Ahh knoooow! Ah, knowww!"—even if she was telling him something that they both thought was unimportant.

"One day, you'll get to meet my brother, Spot," she told her little puppy. "Don't take it personally, boy. He's just . . . distracted sometimes. It doesn't mean he doesn't love you." Rose sighed. Life was best when she could share it with her brother, she thought.

"Careful, Rosie," her father said an hour later as they climbed out of a taxi. "Watch the traffic."

They were in Times Square, and it was just around noon. Normally the traffic in Times Square would have been worth watching, even if her father exaggerated the danger. But after seeing Square Times Square Squared, it was harder to be impressed by old Times Square. True, there were high buildings and bright signs and theater marquees and news zippers racing around . . . but after Square Times Square Squared, it looked pretty small and dingy. And the cars just ran along the street—no violent turns up the sides of buildings and heading toward the sky. Rose, for the first time in her life, actually felt patronizing toward Times Square.

Her father worked here, on the thirtieth floor of a huge tower with an antenna on top. "It looks like the Ministry of Propaganda on Neptune," he'd said mordantly to her mother the first time he had seen it. Her father was a cartoonist for a magazine called *Monocle*, and its offices had once been located in a cozy building downtown. Then *Monocle* had been bought by a big magazine company called Eternal Publications, which in turn had been bought by an even bigger company called Omni Everything, and then Omni Everything had been bought by an even bigger conglomerate called AlphaOmegaMedia. Now, her father worked in the AlphaOmega tower, along with the other writers and cartoonists.

"Choosing cartooning as a way of making a living—now there was one of my brighter choices!" Her father sighed. "A really *booming* field, cartooning. A real growth industry. Boy, was I right about that. Computers, streaming video, computer animation—what could possibly be better than a pen and ink cartoon of two guys on a desert island?" he said as he opened the door to his little office. At least it was bright, and had a nice view of the public library. He sat down at his easel. "Now, what can they be saying to each other this time? 'You forgot the e-mail.' 'Can you get Wi-Fi on a seashell?'"

Her father always drew two kinds of cartoons: either two men stranded on a desert island, in those funny trousers with zigzag hems, saying something to each other, or else there was somebody arriving in heaven and being given a harp, and Saint Peter was saying something to him.

"Long as I have you and Mom and Ollie, kiddo," he said.

Rose gave him a kiss on the cheek, because she knew he appreciated them. He reached out and hugged her.

"Dad, can I go see Mr. Murphy now?" she asked.

He looked up from his drawing board, already absorbed in worrying about his cartoon. "Sure," he said.

Joe Murphy had the office next to her father's. He had written many books about New York—about the waterfront, and the fishermen who still lived there, about strange, hidden stores and weird, unhappy bartenders, and had once been well known. But it had been years since he'd written anything, even though you could still hear his typewriter clacking away in his office when he had the door shut. ("Even AlphaOm can't fire him," her father had explained. "You can't fire a legend.")

Rose loved to visit him. She knocked on his door, and after some shuffling sounds you always hear when an older person is coming to the door, there he was. His face at first wore a puzzled, polite look, but when he saw Rose he broke into a brief, lopsided smile—that kind that shows your molars on one side.

He was a little weird, she thought, but in a nice way. He had the world's most crowded office, filled with paper and old books. But it was only *slightly* smelly, and he loved to talk about New York. He would tell her long stories about all the freaks and oddities and prodigies and eccentrics that he had known in New York as long ago as the nineteen thirties, and she loved to hear his stories: like the one about the bearded lady who lived on Eighty-eighth Street, above a barbershop, and taunted the barbers. Or about the six strange Guarini brothers, who made their living finding lost goods in the tunnels beneath Grand Central Terminal, and about Horace Kingsolver, the great imposter who successfully pretended to be the new conductor of the New York Philharmonic for six straight months in 1939.

"Why, Miss Rose," he said. "To what do I owe the

pleasure?" Even though Joe Murphy had lived in New York for about a century, or so Rose gathered, he still had a soft Southern accent from his hometown of Murgatroyd, North Carolina, a place he often mentioned in conversation.

Rose told him about Professional Day, which was why she had come to the office with her father. "It's sort of like Arch Day," she explained. "When we dance around under this arch. Only without the arch or the dancing."

"I *know*, I *know*," he said, sympathetically. Rose noticed that, as usual, he was wearing a full three-piece suit and tie, even though everyone else in the office wore shirts that hung out around their jeans, and sneakers. The suit had a slightly mothy, out-of-the attic feeling, but it was still a nice suit. "It's fall, and a young woman's fancy, I imagine, turns to thoughts of lunch—of pheasant with chestnuts and turtle soup and walnut cranberry pie?"

Rose bowed. They always had lunch together whenever she visited her father. Usually they just went to the cafeteria, but Mr. Murphy often outlined a bigger meal first.

"Lunch it is!" Mr. Murphy said. "Just wait till I fetch my hat." He always wore a hat to lunch, and then took it off once they got to the table. Rose didn't bother to ask her Dad if she could go to lunch, as it was in the same building.

Upstairs at the cafeteria, it was crowded, and Mr. Murphy

sighed as he took his tray and gave one to Rose.

A chilly hand fell on her from on high. Rose looked and saw that a gleaming diamond bracelet was resting on her shoulder.

"Well, hello, young lady. And with whom are you dining today?"

Rose recognized that the woman with the diamond bracelet and the hand on Rose's shoulder was Ultima Thule. She was the editor of *Madame* magazine, and one of the most famous people in the whole fashion world. She was having lunch with three of her Ultimatums—beautiful, frightened-looking girls who worked for her. People were often frightened of her, Rose knew, but from a distance she had always seemed perfectly nice to Rose.

"Hello, Mr. Murphy," Ultima said now, politely shaking hands with old Joe. "When will you come home and write for *Madame*?"

Rose knew enough to know that if Joe ever did write something, it wouldn't be for *Madame*, but she liked Ultima Thule for being so polite. Joe seemed uncomfortable though, and he introduced Rose. "She's the daughter of Tyrone Parker," he explained.

"Oh, you mean the man with the desert islands? How horribly amusing" was all Ultima Thule said. You couldn't see her eyes behind the sunglasses she always wore.

Rose didn't know how to respond, so she said, "I saw that article about your dollhouse collection." She really had seen a story about Ultima's dollhouse collection once in *Madame*. "The collection looked extremely beautiful."

"Well, come up to my office sometime," Ultima said kindly. "I have Florine Stettheimer's last dollhouse. It's a wonder."

Rose said she would, and Ultima wandered off with her little clique.

Rose glanced around the cafeteria and realized it was full of people she knew through her father. Usually it was great, but today she just wanted to be alone with Mr. Murphy so that she could show him the dog in her pocket and tell him about U Nork without anyone overhearing. She looked up at Mr. Murphy and found him searching the hot tables of the cafeteria with a long, melancholy look. Everywhere there was arugula and mesclun and little pieces of grilled chicken and tofu.

She had an idea.

"Mr. Murphy," she said, "I guess we should make up a good healthy salad for lunch. I see they have lots of organic steamed broccoli today. . . ."

There must have been something about the way she said "steamed organic broccoli" that made him decide.

"Miss Rose," he said slowly. "I'm not a man who looks

askance at Nature's bounty. But here we see around us an undue, I mean a positively un*due* concentration on what you might call the healthful side of Nature, and not enough on what you might call the succulent side.

"What would you say," Mr. Murphy went on, "what would you say to adjourning our luncheon to the Oyster Bar at the Grand Central Terminal, where you and I, Miss Rose, might dine on oyster pan roasts made the right way, with heavy cream and plump bluepoints trucked in fresh from the Island, and some red pepper, and just the right amount of Worcestershire sauce, and maybe a flaky biscuit or two to sop up the sauce? And maybe leave the tofu to what you might, uh, call the, uh, surrounding tofites?" The way he said it made Rose hungry.

That was *exactly* what Rose had been hoping for! Her plan had worked. She knew that she ought to ask her dad if she could leave the office, but this was too good a chance. So she just said yes, and they were off. She hoped her dad wouldn't worry about where she was if he found out she had left the building.

It was funny, and sort of nice, to be walking on the street on a fall day with Mr. Murphy. He was a slow walker, like most old people, but it wasn't because his legs didn't work well. He was just a *careful* walker, and Rose had the impression that he had probably walked that way when he was younger, stepping over cracks and dog poop with real care, and always looking up at the second stories of buildings and down at their basement entrances. The shadows of fall cast nice long lines across his face, and as they walked he talked gaily about old times in New York.

"Now, right here," he would say, pointing to some big fifty-story glass tower, "why, that's where old Mr. Rattle kept the best speakeasy in New York. In 1928 it opened. It was such a pleasing kind of place that, even after Prohibition was over, his customers continued to pretend that drinking was illegal, just to add the thrill of lawbreaking to the pleasure of whiskey. He used to hire unemployed men to dress up like policemen and raid the place. I should *write* something about all that," he said sorrowfully.

"And over there, way down there, why"—his brow crinkled—"that was the very basement nightclub where the great Prez Young first played that swoop of his on the tenor sax; 1942, that happened. He was shelling a peanut in his teeth, and the shell went down the wrong way, and he just kinda coughed into his horn, and there it was, that beautiful swoop." He held his hands up like a man playing a saxophone, slightly sideways and in distress. "And by the weekend, every two-bit, uh, lesser tenor man on Fifty-second street was doing it, too. Without knowing that you needed the peanut shell for the full effect." He paused for thought. "I should *write* somethin' about that, too," he said at last, even more mournfully.

Rose looked at the place that he was pointing toward. It was another fifty-story glass tower.

"Do you miss the old New York, Mr. Murphy?" she asked. It must be hard to always be surrounded by ghosts and memories, she thought. She asked him on tiptoes—not actual tiptoes, but the sort of mental tiptoes you go up on when you're asking someone a sensitive or personal question.

Mr. Murphy stopped walking. "Miss it?" He thought it over. "No, I don't *miss* it exactly. I *remember* it. It's still in my mind, which is where all good things go to live after they've died in this world. In your mind, that is. The biggest nation in the world is the *imagination*, as my dad used to tell me in Murgatroyd, North Carolina. When he was, well, sober enough to give advice." He looked appealingly at Rose, as though he hoped she wouldn't blame him for being candid about his father.

"Anyway, there are still plenty of old places where an old dog like me can find a dog dish. Like the Grand Central Oyster Bar."

Rose had been once to the Oyster Bar with her father, and she had liked it. It was a long, low cellar room, covered with weaving tiles and with a long counter snaking through it. There were tables with red-checkered tablecloths, but everyone who knew what was what sat at the counter, which was where Rose and Mr. Murphy now sat, too. Rose liked underground rooms and low ceilings. She must have been a lizard or something in an earlier life, she thought.

They ordered their pan roasts. As they ate the spicy, rich stew—Rose didn't actually eat the oysters, which she found too hard to chew, but she liked all the surrounding bits—she tried to find the right way to tell Mr. Murphy about U Nork. But it seemed too awkward, and anyway, not really believable.

He seemed relaxed, and she was glad to see that he wasn't one of those old people who sort of slurped his food and showed his teeth and gums while he did it. He could talk and eat at the same time without being sloppy. Rose wished there were more old people like that.

"The thing about this city," he was saying, "is that it's full of hiding places. Why does it feel so right to be in an oyster bar? Because we're all oysters here, livin' in our shells! You're an oyster! I'm an oyster! All clammed up inside our shells, working on our pearls.

"Why, I knew someone who lived right here in the terminal, stowed away in a little apartment he found up hidden in the ceiling. Other people live down below, in

the tunnels. Why, even a man living in a one-room studio has more of a universe to himself than anyone could
in Murgatroyd! In small towns, you never have your own
world, no matter how much space you have. In cities,
there's a world in every room. Here in New York, it's secret
upon secret upon secret! World upon world upon world!
Why, no—a universe! A galaxy! Anything you like, all in a
tiny space." He smiled.

"Mr. Murphy," Rose said, once she thought of a way
to raise the issue on her mind without giving away the
truth. "Mr. Murphy, where would you go if you needed
information on, uh, something weird? A bit weird. Like,
you know—intergalactic travel of entire civilizations from
one planet to the next? And, uh, the care and feeding of
super-tiny dogs?"

He didn't even stir from his pan roast when she said
it. "Intergalactic travel? Care of hyper-miniaturized dogs?
Well, for out-of-the way information and good old books
that have it, the only place to go is the Medusa bookstore,
and ask the Cone sisters."

"Where's that?" Rose asked.

For the first time, Mr. Murphy looked genuinely surprised. "Medusa Books? You mean your father's never
taken you there? Well, that's a long overdue polka on your
dance card, Miss Rose. What do you say"—he furrowed his

brow again, as he always did when he was proposing to do something, in his slightly long-winded way—"what do you say we adjourn there after a slice or two of Key lime pie and coffee or a glass of milk, and you meet the Cone girls?"

Mr. Murphy insisted on paying the bill, and a few moments later they were back outside the great station, slowly walking north along Lexington Avenue toward Fifty-ninth Street. Rose knew that she really ought to call her father and tell him where she was, but this was too important.

"Shouldn't we take a subway?" Rose asked. "Or maybe a bus?" Mr. Murphy was moving along very slowly.

"Subways are for families. And buses are for old people. That leaves walking for real New Yorkers like you and me, Miss Rose."

It was nice, though, because all the while they walked, Mr. Murphy kept pointing out secret places and forgotten locales on the avenue. "Always look at the basements and the second floor in a big city," he advised her. "That's where the real life is. The newcomers are living in the basements, and the old trades are practiced on the upper floors." He pointed them out: a dance studio on the second floor above a deli, where you could see Latinos practicing the tango; a door that led upstairs to a Chinese newspaper; a lodge of Elks ("That's a kind of club," he explained); and a little square manhole ("That's just for the electrical company to get down to the lines. They don't want too many people to know that there's an easy way to get down there!"). And way up high, a magic store ("They used to own the whole building," he said. "But now they've retreated into one story"). It was funny, Rose thought, walking with Mr. Murphy in New York just a few hours after walking with Louis through U Nork; in U Nork all she could see was the big stuff, and here in New York all she could pay attention to was the little stuff.

Rose thought all of this was interesting, but she was feeling a bit impatient, too. She was desperate to show Mr. Murphy Spot, but she needed to find a secluded place to do it.

It was especially frustrating when they stopped to look in the window of Pets on Lex, where Rose could see the happy Havanese and Maltese puppies jumping and playing. She took Mr. Murphy's hand in excitement, and secretly reached her other hand into her coat pocket, just to make sure that Spot was still safe. Yes, she could still feel him wriggling happily in her pocket. . . .

"I had a dog once," Mr. Murphy was saying. "A beagle, he was. A Carolina beagle . . ."

Then Rose saw something alarming reflected in the pet store window. She wheeled around.

"Look!" Rose cried.

It was the pink limousine, crawling down Lexington Avenue, slowing as it drove by the pair of them, and in the backseat, those catlike eyes glowing through the tinted window.

"Look!" she cried again. But Mr. Murphy took so long to turn around that he missed it. Whoever it was in the car had been looking at them, Rose was sure of it. And when she turned around again, it was gone—the entire long pink limousine had vanished.

A Store and a Prison

At last they reached Medusa Books. It was a handsome six-story building, and on its roof a brave banner blew in the wind. On the banner Medusa herself was staring down and reading a book, and some of the snake heads had started reading the book too. Rose guessed that her teacher would say that it showed even weird things can be civilized by literature. But it was a cool banner.

The store itself would have seemed like quite a large store in most places, but here on this block, with fifty-story black glass towers surrounding it on all sides, it looked small and brave and defiant.

"Yes," Mr. Murphy said, "this is the last real bookstore. The Cone girls inherited it from their father, Sid. They keep getting offers to sell it, but they won't. When they do, the city will be finished," he ended flatly, then added, with a bit more sparkle, "and so will I, Rose, so will I. Anyway, whatever out-of-the way information you're looking for, you'll find it here."

Rose nodded politely. She supposed that Mr. Murphy had never heard of Google or the Internet, and how you could search for anything that way instantly, including cool pictures of little dogs. If Oliver had let her do a Google search that morning, she might already have found out what Spot ate.

"I know they have these new whatdayacallems, online searches," Mr. Murphy said, with quiet dignity, as they passed by the outside bookcases and walked in the door, as though he'd read her mind. "But what do they do, Rose? They put together the most popular writings on a subject and put them in a list. That's what comes up first. Here, the Cone sisters will find you the most *unpopular* writings on the most unknown subjects. Now, which is more useful for someone who wants real knowledge?"

They went into the store together. It had the good smell of old paper, which lined the room from floor to ceiling. Extra books were piled high all around. Among the piles, Rose could *just* see the tops of three women's heads. They must be sitting at desks a few feet apart, she thought, but all you could see was their hair and the frames of their glasses, which rested on top of their heads.

"Norma, didn't I tell you that the last volume was mis-shelved. It got misshelved in 1967, and we've just found it again. . . ."

Mr. Murphy raised his hat tentatively, and, as though they had antennae that responded to any movement of air in the bookstore, all three sisters suddenly stood up. All three had the kind of old-fashioned glasses that dangle from long ribbons; all three had bright, frowning faces; and all three now looked directly at Rose. They seemed very glad to see Mr. Murphy, and then they introduced themselves to Rose as Norma, Alexandra, and Cynthia. Rose realized at once that she would never be able to tell them apart, and that she would just have to nod politely and find ways of starting sentences that didn't need the person's name at the beginning. Fortunately, each one wore glasses whose frame was of a slightly different color and design.

Mr. Murphy said, "Rose here is looking for some special information, some book on some subject, and I told her that you ladies were, uh, the only ones who could help her."

"Yes, what is it?" one of them asked.

"Uh—the care and feeding of super-small dogs?" Rose said, adding a question mark sound to the end of her sentence, because she knew it sounded so stupid.

But the Cone sisters didn't flinch or smile or raise their eyebrows.

The one who seemed oldest spoke first. "How small? This small?" She held her hands about two feet apart. Her glasses were dark brown tortoiseshell.

"This small?" the next sister asked, and she held out her hands about a foot apart. Her glasses had sky blue frames, and the lenses were tinted blue as well.

"Or this small?" the last one asked, holding her hands about six inches apart. *Her* glasses, tilted up high on her head, were a warm red, like the color of a sunset.

"Well, more like this small," Rose said, and she reluctantly took Spot out of her pocket. He blinked in the light of the bookstore.

"That *is* small," the sister with the blue frames said. "Quite small. We will have to look in rare books!" she added, not seeming the least bit startled by Spot's small size.

The one with tortoiseshell glasses was already searching through the card catalogue beside her. "Hyper-tiny pets? We had something on that—Cynthia, where did that care and feeding book go?"

Rose was surprised. She had expected them to be shocked at the request, but they weren't. They were rummaging through piles of books, and old paper, and ancient magazines, and all the other material filling the floor of the bookstore.

Meanwhile, Mr. Murphy was scrutinizing Spot, who sat quietly in Rose's hand. Spot seemed very subdued, Rose thought. He must be hungry, and she still didn't know what to feed him!

"Is it under here? I *know* we had that book. I saw it, oh, yesterday. Either yesterday or fifteen years ago. Sometimes it's hard to tell in a bookstore."

"Definitely not fifteen years ago. That I would remember," said the one with sky-blue glasses. "I always remember things that happened fifteen years ago."

"Where was it published? Do you remember that?"

Alexandra frowned. "London? Hong Kong? Maybe Mars?"

The other sisters frowned, too, trying to remember. Rose was startled to hear them talk about publishing on Mars as though it was the most normal thing in the world.

"Maybe it's upstairs . . ." the one in red glasses brooded. "Come with me! We keep all the paraphernalia upstairs."

There was a small hand-operated elevator in the rear of the store, and she and Rose got on it. The cage door shut, and she worked the lever that brought the elevator up, in short jerks. Then Rose and the red-framed Cone sister got off on the third floor. Instead of being filled with books, it was filled with strange old dusty objects and maps that hung everywhere on the wall, old prints, and ancient recruiting posters, with Uncle Sam pointing and the writing I WANT YOU! below.

"I *know* we had all the old files up here," the Cone sister said with what sounded like annoyance.

"Don't you think you should turn on the lights?" Rose asked. It was extremely dark up on this floor.

Cynthia—for that's who Rose decided she was—looked at her as though she were Leonardo da Vinci himself.

"What a *good* idea!" she said, and she went over toward the wall, groping for the light switch. "You know," she said cheerfully, "I'm so used to feeling my way around here in the dark that I don't even bother with the lights sometimes. Now, where's that switch?"

As Rose's eyes adjusted to the darkness, she could see something gleaming in a remote corner. Several somethings, actually. Round glass edges, catching the little bit of daylight that came in through the shutter-bound windows of the third floor. There was something alluring about them . . . something oddly familiar.

Rose started to approach them. Cynthia, seeing her move forward in the darkness, suddenly called out to her. "Rose, don't go there!"

But just as she said this, the lights all came on at once. The entire floor filled with a bright, harsh radiance. And Rose could see that the part of the old wooden floor that she had been walking toward was covered with ugly looking shards and pieces of broken glass—some of it piled up in a little heap, and some left lying loose on the floor.

"We keep intending to clean that up," red-framed Cynthia said, hurriedly. And then she said—suddenly harsh—"No. The old cards aren't up here at all. I forgot." She hustled the curious Rose back into the elevator, and was silent all the way down.

When they got back to the first floor, Mr. Murphy was sitting on the edge of one of the desks having an intense conversation with the two remaining Cone sisters.

"I can't find it," Cynthia told him sharply. "It's not up there. You two had better go. We have work to do."

Mr. Murphy gave Rose a puzzled look. "What *happened* up there?" it seemed to say.

"But I'm sure that the old slips are up there," Alexandra said, looking just as puzzled as Mr. Murphy. "Cynthia, you must have—"

"I *said* they're not there," Cynthia said sharply again. "They're just not there. Now, sisters, we have some, um, important work to do. We'd better get on with it." She gave Mr. Murphy and Rose a don't-you-think-you're-overstaying-your-welcome? look. And soon Rose, Mr. Murphy, and Spot, who was back in Rose's pocket, were all out on the street again.

"Honestly, Mr. Murphy, all there was was some broken *glass* up there," said Rose. "Really, that's, like, all. And I started walking over to look at it, and she got well, not upset exactly. *Worried*, more."

Rose and Mr. Murphy walked slowly back toward the AlphaOmega Building. Mr. Murphy had been very silent since they left Medusa Books. He was listening intently now as Rose explained what had happened—or, more like, what hadn't happened—to change Cynthia Cone's mood so quickly.

"Rose," Mr. Murphy said, and looked at her quizzically. He seemed almost ready to say something, but then seemed to think better of it. He shook his head. And then he said at last, "Rose—where did you get that li'l dog?"

He was looking at her very searchingly.

One part of Rose wished that she could tell him all about U Nork, and what she had seen there, and how she had gone there, and how Spot came from there.

But how could she be really sure that Mr. Murphy wouldn't think she was a little crazy? To be honest, she sometimes thought that *he* was a little crazy. There's a difference between trusting someone enough to go to lunch with them in broad daylight without telling your dad, and trusting someone enough to tell them a bizarre-yet-true story about an enormous buried city and a tiny dog.

Anyway, something inside her kept Rose from doing it. It was as if . . . she wasn't really ready yet. After all, she hadn't even told *Oliver*.

"At a pet store," she said finally, her lips tight. "I bought him at a pet store. Up on Lexington Avenue. Not Pets on Lex. Another one. Lex Pets, it's called. He was a, sort of a freak. No one wanted him, so I bought him." Rose was a pretty good liar, and she thought this was a pretty good lie.

Mr. Murphy looked at her, hard. "Are you sure, Rose, that—" he began. But then he caught himself. "Okay, Rose," he said at last. "Whatever you tell me, I'll believe." And he looked at her hard again.

Rose understood that he was saying more than he seemed to be saying. He was saying that if she told him the truth he would accept that, and if she didn't tell him the truth, he would accept that too—which was really an invitation to tell him the truth about U Nork! But since she was already on the record with a lie, she might seem a little unreliable if she immediately changed it to the truth. So she just kept her lips shut tight and nodded.

She still didn't know what to feed Spot!

When they got back to the twentieth floor at last, Mr. Murphy, still very silent, said a little dreamily, "It might be worth makin' another visit there sometime, Rose." Then he firmly shut the door to his office.

Another visit *where*? Rose wondered.

Her father was still working on the cartoon of the two men on the desert island. He was bent over his drawing board and had his old Walkman on, with the headphones pressed to his ears. When he saw Rose, he smiled and blew her a kiss—apparently he was so distracted by his work that he hadn't even noticed she'd been away for two and a half hours!

She heard a tiny whimper. She reached into her pocket to take out poor hungry Spot.

"Are you ready to see my house?" a cool voice said suddenly.

Rose's heart leaped into her throat, and she thrust Spot back into her pocket just in time.

It was Ultima. But why was she lingering around her father's remote office?

"I came to find you," the woman almost cooed. "To see if you would like to see that dollhouse. . . ."

"Uh—sure," Rose said. "I'd be very happy to see your collection." And then she added, "I collect snow globes, you see." When she said it, she just wanted to sort of increase their mutual interests, but it was actually a kind of random and off-topic thing to add, she realized, as soon as it was out. But Ultima turned on her heel, and looked very hard at her. And then Rose followed Ultima out of the office and down in the elevator to *Madame* magazine.

To her shock, Mr. Murphy was there, too—right in Ultima's enormous, gray-carpeted office. It was at least twenty times bigger than her father's little office, and even had two flat-screen televisions and a fridge.

Mr. Murphy was sitting slumped down in an armchair, looking distracted and unhappy.

"Rose, my dear," Ultima said, nicely—though Ultima's nice sounded like most people's icy. "Come—sit down. Take off your coat and leave it here. The dollhouse is in the other room."

Rose looked at Mr. Murphy, but for some reason he was shy about looking at her now. She nodded, hesitantly.

"Mr. Murphy and I were just beginning to have a little chat about you," Ultima said. That alarmed Rose. Suddenly she was glad she hadn't told him about U Nork! "My assistant, Penultima, here, will show you the dollhouse, while Mr. Murphy and I finish our conversation. Just leave your coat, dear," she added insinuatingly.

Rose wanted to be polite. But she also didn't want to leave her coat with Spot in the pocket. So she carefully put her coat down on the chair that Ultima had gestured to, while at the same time quietly reaching into the pocket and cupping Spot inconspicuously in her palm while turning the back of her hand toward the grown-ups (sometimes it is very useful to have a brother who is a magician and teaches you stuff).

Penultima, Rose saw, was slightly taller and much gawkier than Ultima. She stood off to one side of the office, wearing a black suit with gold piping on the seams (Ultima's suit was gold with black piping on the seams; that was nicer, Rose thought). Rose followed her into the next room.

The amazing dollhouse sat in the corner of a small room—a sort of library, Rose thought—that adjoined Ultima's enormous office. The dollhouse was eight stories tall—taller than Rose, actually—and had been wedged into the corner, so that it looked as if you could only walk around it by squeezing through a tiny space behind. That didn't matter; there was plenty to look at on its open side.

It *was* amazing. Every bit of furniture was lacquered and finished. It was all done in a modern style, with chrome and leather and beautiful painted wood, and the paintings on the walls were beautiful tiny paintings, obviously done by real artists. Rose knelt and looked at it with fascination.

The phone rang. Penultima went to get it. "Yes, Howell. . . ." She looked at Rose. She seemed uncertain about what to do. "Yes, I'll be right there," she said into the phone. "Dear, I'm going to leave you for just a second," she said to Rose, and then was gone.

Rose kept looking at the dollhouse. She still had Spot palmed in her hand, so she released the pressure on him, for fear that she might be squeezing out all his air.

Oh, good! He was fine, she realized as she opened her hand. In a flash, he leaped to the ground and ran inside the dollhouse, looking back at Rose as though playfully daring her to chase him.

Naughty dog! Rose thought with affection. He must be hungry, and yet he still wanted to play. She bent down to take him out of the dollhouse.

She reached inside. But Spot wasn't there. She peered through the doorway. No, he wasn't . . . but she could hear his tiny bark, growing ever fainter as she searched for him. Where had he gone?

She looked inside. There! She could just see him . . . he seemed to have run deep into the dollhouse, right to the back part that was set up against the wall. Oh, dear . . . Rose got up.

She saw, as she had when she came into the room, that there was just barely space enough between the wall and the house for her to squeeze in. It looked uncomfortable . . . but she absolutely couldn't lose Spot in there. She slipped

along the wall, making herself as sideways as she could. She could see that this part of the dollhouse was open, too, and full of other rooms—sort of like the poor relations' wing. She realized that if she kneeled down, she was small enough to be able to wedge inside the narrow space and look at the hidden side of the house.

She did, and though it was a very tight fit, she bent down eagerly to see if she could find Spot. There he was! Good dog, having raced all the way right through the house, as though looking for the back garden. She scooped him up. Now she'd just take a peek at the treasures in that hidden part of the house. . . .

She gasped.

This other side of the dollhouse was nothing like the front.

She stared with horror. It was a warren of small prison cells, hundreds of them, stacked one on top of the next. Each one had a small metal bed, a gray blanket, and a window—with bars on it. And a metal door with a single tiny opening in it, which swung on a tiny, delicate, miniature hinge. She reached out and touched one lightly with a finger. The little metal door swung shut delicately, and then slammed home, tight.

Hundreds and hundreds of secret small prison cells on the hidden side of the dollhouse!

She heard footsteps returning, and, picking Spot up on her thumb, Rose scrambled back out from behind the dollhouse into the little room.

Ultima Thule was standing there. "Ah, Rose," she said, looking at her with dark suspicion. "Have you been enjoying the house?" She had Penultima beside her, who seemed crestfallen and disturbed. Then Rose noticed that she held Rose's coat over her right arm. And that the pockets had been turned inside out.

Rose nodded. Feeling very frightened, she decided that she *had* to get away from Ultima and Penultima, the creepy dollhouse, and the suddenly silent Mr. Murphy. She grabbed the coat from Penultima's arm, called out a quick, "Thank you very much for letting me look. I'm late!" and fled—running all the way out of the offices of *Madame*, back out into the corridor, and onto the elevator that took her back to her father's office.

Chapter Seven

THE WRONG SIDE OF THE STREET

"It was *freakish*, that's what it was," Rose was saying to Oliver a few hours later. "It was just freakish. She had all these little tiny cells ready for . . . someone."

"Who knows, Rosie." Oliver shrugged. "Maybe she likes to, I don't know, imprison her dolls. Tie them up and put handcuffs on them. Fashion people are weird."

"This wasn't weird. This was *freakish*. Rumpelstiltskin-quality freakish." Rose always thought that Rumpelstiltskin was a kind of gold standard for freakishness—that weird little guy stamping his foot and sneaking into the queen's room at night.

"Are you still scared of Rumpelstiltskin?" Oliver asked.

"I'm not scared of anything, in particular."

She was almost bursting at this point to tell Oliver all about U Nork, and the steps across the water—but something held her back. The fear of ridicule, of course—she didn't want her brother to laugh at her; she wanted her brother to admire her for being so brave—but also another kind of feeling. The sense that whatever had brought her to U Nork, whatever it was that made its citizens hang giant banners of her in Square Times Square Squared, was something she would have to understand for herself first.

She heard a tiny whimper. Spot! He hadn't eaten all day or, well, done anything else either. He was going to be sick! She had tried Googling on her mother's computer, but there didn't seem to be a single Web page about the care of thumbnail-size dogs.

She had to go back to U Nork, if only to find out what to feed her puppy!

So that night, Rose knew she had to go out again to the steps across the water. This time she would have to go out very late. She hoped the steps would still be waiting in the park. She pulled her violet coat over her Chinese pajamas and waited until her mother, father, and even Oliver was asleep.

But how was she going to get out? The doorman, Leon, who stood all night downstairs, was very nice, but if he saw her sneaking out after midnight, he would certainly call up to her parents. And then what?

Rose stood by the front door and brooded. Then an idea came to her. She walked softly into her room and took out a piece of paper from her notepad—the sheet had pink-haired fairies and unicorns on it—that she'd gotten for her birthday from her grandmother. It was extremely cheesy, but it was the only loose paper she had. She scribbled something on one sheet, then she went to the intercom by the front door.

Leon picked up. "Yes!" he said, sounding very excited. She supposed that he waited all night down there, hoping something interesting would happen.

"Leon," she said. "This is Rose in 6A. There are strange noises up here. I think something strange is happening. Can you come up right away?"

"Okay! Be right there!" he said.

Of course, he could have asked her why she didn't wake up her parents, but he hadn't. Maybe he wanted something interesting to do.

Rose quickly walked outside, taped the message onto the front of the door, shut it as silently as she could, then hid in the alcove of the service elevator door, right across the hall. From there, she could watch the apartment door without being seen.

Sure enough, moments later, Leon the night doorman

in his handsome semi-military uniform, came racing from the elevator toward their front door. Rose crossed her fingers nervously. She hoped he would be enterprising but not too enterprising.

Leon drew close to the door and peered at the paper, on which she'd written:

PROBLEM SOLVED!
BUT GO CHECK WITH 8A
THE PROBLEM MAY BE THERE NOW!

Don't knock! Rose prayed under her breath.

But he didn't. Instead, Leon did exactly what she'd hoped he'd do. He got a very serious look, held his handsome visored hat down, and raced down the hall to the fire exit. In a moment, Rose could hear him clattering up the stairs.

Now! Rose thought.

She ripped the note from the door—she didn't want her parents finding it in the morning or anything—stuffed it in her coat pocket, and ran for the elevator. She knew that the older couple who lived in 8A would take about a million years to wake up and put on their bathrobes after Leon knocked on the door—when you went trick-or-treating at their apartment on Halloween it took them days just to find the Snickers bars in the basket right by their door—so

Rose would probably have five minutes before he came back down.

The elevator seemed to take forever—on a school morning, of course, it went as fast as, well, as fast as a U Nork elevator—but before long, there she was in the lobby and racing for the front door. She had a bad moment when she realized that Leon had locked it, but then she saw that he had only locked it from the inside. All she had to do was turn the bolt, and she was out!

Rose ran all the way to the park, through the dark and the mysterious streets, her violet coat pulled tight around her Chinese pajamas. She ran past all the familiar monuments of her neighborhood—past the Guggenheim Museum, which looked like a huge white cone of soft-swirl ice cream, and the Metropolitan Museum, which looked like a long giant temple with great steps leading up to it.

Racing in darkness across the empty lawn, with the leaves rustling all around her, Rose saw the place where she had first seen the steps rising up near the turtle pond. She got there and waited for them to appear.

Then, from across the lawn, two bright lights like searchlights suddenly stung her eyes. They seemed to be moving toward her, and she realized they were car headlights. She could just make out, in the rapidly approaching white light, the shape and tint of the pink limousine.

And they were coming directly at Rose. She could see eyes inside: two catlike eyes of a woman, and more eyes, too, frightening yellow ones. . . .

Where were the steps?

The car made an angry growl as it sped across the grass at her . . . and then suddenly stopped. The door opened, and two dogs came leaping out of the backseat, their eyes yellow with rage—frightening eyes—barking the high-pitched snarls of wild jackals. They jumped and howled as they ran across the lawn toward her. . . .

There! The glass stair was stretching across the pond again, and Rose raced up it with all the speed she could muster. With terror, she heard the first wild dog dash onto the steps behind her, growling and barking fiercely—but the smooth glass surface made his claws scrabble and slip. There was a momentary whimper as he worked his paws to grab hold. Spot whined in her pocket. Rose went up the stairs as fast as she could, but her feet felt like syrup.

Now she was up and almost over them, and once again she shut her eyes as she leaped for the far side just as she felt the hot breath of the wild dog on her hand. She stretched back to try and protect herself. The two lights of the limousine were trained directly on her, as though they were searchlights and she an escaping prisoner.

Silence.

Then a roar.

Rose opened her eyes, terrified of finding the hungry eyes and slavering jaws of the wild dog above her.

But all she saw were the high towers and bright golden sunlight of a U Nork street, with zeppelins and pigeons like tiny moving dots in the blue sky above, and a boy's face looking quizzically down at her.

"Hey. Looks like you're on the wrong side of the street, lady."

Rose pulled herself up on one elbow. The bright light, evenly spread, dazed her eyes. There were the towers, and the flags fluttering high. . . .

"You're on the wrong side of the street, lady," the boy repeated.

"Oh," she said. It was odd being called "lady" by a boy her age. "Yeah, I guess I am." She got up slowly and blinked her eyes. "Where, exactly, am I?" she asked.

The boy peered more carefully at her. "It's Rose!" he cried suddenly. "Oh, my goodness. What are *you* doing on the wrong side of the street?" He seemed worried for her. All around her the great throng of U Nork went past, stepping lightly and walking rapidly, the women's high heels clacking on the ground and the men growling and gesticulating to each other as they walked.

"Why is it the wrong side?" Rose asked.

"Because you're in the kitchen instead of the dining room," the boy explained. He was wearing the white uniform of an outdoor café cook. Only, instead of having on a high white chef's hat, he had on a little white skullcap. His face was drawn and sort of scraggly, but his eyes were shining and intelligent.

"I'm blue," he added, simply.

"I'm sorry to hear it," Rose said, trying to be as polite as she could. "Why?"

"Oh," he laughed. "No! I mean, that's my name, Blue. Blue Boghen."

"Hey, Blue," Rose said. By now she was feeling better and had looked around. She realized the great café across the street was where she had had that hurried lunch with Louis.

"I work one of the mayonnaise cannons," Blue explained.

"Oh, you mean you shoot the sauce directly in people's mouths?" Rose said, with a slight shudder. That had been a fairly gross experience.

"Yeah," the boy said agreeably, "but it takes a lot of training to learn how to aim the cannons just right."

"I hadn't thought of that. . . ."

"Of course you hadn't. No one ever does," Blue said, with just a trace of resentment. "People just think, 'Oh,

I'll have a leisurely five-minute lunch.' No one ever thinks about the poor boys working the sauce cannon across the street. If you hit someone in the eye or something, you could really injure them—so I'm just an apprentice. Learning to load mayonnaise, aim mayonnaise, fire mayonnaise . . . They'll put me on the mustard guns next, and then I may get my chance at the béarnaise battery. When he was a kid, my dad was the best . . ." Blue broke off suddenly.

Sauce cannons were being loaded just over Rose's head. Everyone was working hard—really sweating with the effort. One of the young under-chefs in a white coat was regimenting the others. His skullcap was bright gold.

"Up! Aim! Fire mayonnaise!" he called, and right on cue, a spray of creamy sauce crossed the street into the mouth of a waiting diner.

"Wow," Rose said. It was somehow much more impressive seeing this done than having it done to you. "What do you use to fire them, Blue? Gunpowder?"

"Gunpowder! Naah—that would burn the sauce. No, some of the sauce cannons are aimed with compressed air, and some with springs. I work the compressed air cannons—you have to work them with your arms to get enough air into them. I'm just on a break—thirty seconds for lunch. I better hurry back."

"It looks like hard work," Rose said sympathetically.

"Yeah, it can hurt your arms," Blue agreed. "But you have to be careful. If you pump in too much air, you could hurt someone, but if you don't pump in enough, the sauce just puddles in the middle of the street. I'm getting good at it—sometimes I think I could point the cannon straight up and shoot a hot steak to the moon!" He sounded very serious.

Then he perked up. "But you're . . . Rose!" he repeated. "Rose, right here on the wrong side of the street." His face shone with excitement, and Rose felt a little guilty. She was still just Rose . . .

"I'm looking for Louis . . ." She stopped when she realized that she didn't know Louis's last name. "You know, the very talkative little person? I mean, little man." (She had watched enough television to know that it was rude and insensitive to call a midget "a midget.") "He's friends with the mayor," she added, a little lamely.

"Sure! Everyone knows Louis. I mean, I don't *know* him or anything. But I know who he *is*. He usually comes round for lunch—he spends two or three minutes here, you know, a big deal. Boy, lucky guy—he can afford it!"

"I need to find him. Could you help me call a pigeon?" She was beginning to learn her way around U Nork.

"Sure thing!" Blue said, and he stuck a hand straight up, calling a pigeon. But none appeared. Then, to impress

her, Rose thought, he reached up again, waving both hands. As he did, there was a clatter of cutlery and a rush of soft sounds. From the pocket of his uniform she saw a little pile of half-eaten food—pieces of hot dogs, chips, and stale bread—fall to the ground.

Blue looked up at her, terrified. "Don't tell anyone!" he said. "Don't tell anyone, please!"

"Tell them what?" Rose puzzled.

"About . . . all that. The food. Please don't tell them that I'm keeping food." He drew close to her. "It's for my dad. He's in . . ." Blue Boghen looked wildly around and then drew close and whispered to her. "He's in . . . Central Park."

Rose of course felt sorry for Blue. It must be very painful to have a father who was homeless and everything, and living in the park.

At that very moment, darkness fell over the block, like a shadow, as though a cloud had eclipsed the sun. Spot stirred in her pocket and let out the saddest, meekest little whine Rose had ever heard.

Rose lifted Spot from her pocket and kissed him right on his tiny little forehead. "It's okay, Spot. We'll get you food soon, boy."

Blue seemed surprised at first. Almost shocked, really. Then he laughed, even though his eyes still looked worried.

"Is he . . . okay?"

"He's really hungry," she began, "and I don't know what to feed him." Her voice sounded frantic.

"Rose . . . that's a Norky! A purebred Norky! You don't see one of those every day!"

"Oh!" she said. So *that's* what Spot was. A Norky! She loved the sound of it. "Do you think you could spare a tiny bit of those scraps for him?"

"Rose, Norkies don't eat scraps. They eat—"

Suddenly, a woman screamed in fear. Rose could sense people's heads shooting up, as though on springs.

She also looked up. There in the sky were two enormous glowing eyes—the cat's eyes she had seen in the back of the limousine. Only now they filled the sky and seemed to be staring directly at her.

"Surrender the stone!" came a voice directly out of the sky. "Surrender the stone and you may live. . . ." The voice had a silvery, threatening tinkle, like the sound of ten thousand icicles breaking all at once.

"Alma!" Blue's voice was hushed with wonder. "It is Alma the Ice Queen! But you're . . . you're here, Rose!"

"Surrender the diamond!" the voice intoned. "Surrender the diamond—or watch your city fall!"

All the traffic on U Nork Avenue stopped, the cars screeching to a frightened halt. Rose heard a few crashes in the distance. The men and women on the street fell to their knees with fear.

And then Rose heard her own name being called out of the sky!

"Rose!" the voice cried. "Rose! Leave now! Go home—and go home soon! The end of the city is near! There is no answer! There can never be an answer! There is no answer to be found!"

"Hey! Rose is here! Rose is here!" a man began to call out on the street, where the people cowered in the darkness. "Have no fear! Rose is here!" And he reached to pull her up, so that everyone could see her. "Rose is here! She's not afraid of you! Rose is here. Rose for U Nork!"

And the crowds on the street, who had fallen to their knees and begun to crouch in fear, slowly stood and went to where Blue held Rose's hand. And then, to Rose's great confusion, they lifted her up onto their shoulders and began to shout at the great eyes in the sky.

"Rose is here! Rose is here! She's not afraid! She ain't afraid!"

"Yeah! She ain't afraid of the Ice Queen!"

"Yeah! Show her! Show her, Rose!" someone else cried.

Rose didn't know what to do. Nervously she reached into her coat to feel for Spot. She hoped he wasn't scared.

She felt something else in her pocket. She took it out.

It was the sheet of cheesy notepaper that she had put on the apartment door, then stuffed into her coat as she ran from the apartment. PROBLEM SOLVED . . .

Before she knew what was happening, a man grabbed it from her with glee. He read it quickly, and then waved it back and forth above his head.

"Problem solved!" he shouted. "Problem solved! Rose says that the problem's solved!"

"Not exactly, no," Rose started to say. "*Please* give that back."

But soon a whole mob of U Norkers—men in hats, women in suits and high heels, children in knickers—was dancing around Rose's notepaper.

"Problem solved! Problem solved!" they cried together, as loud as they could, and Rose could see how delighted and relieved they were. They passed the paper back and forth, like the Stanley Cup, and held it up to the sky, as though to defy the giant sinister eyes.

"Problem solved! Problem solved!" they shouted and danced.

Rose still tried to get it back. She was worried someone would open it and find out it was just a cheap way of fooling Leon and getting out of the apartment building.

In fact, someone did open it up. Rose gulped. A man in a fedora hat saw that it was folded over, and he opened it wide. There was a silent pause on the dark street.

"Look!" he said in wonder. "Problem solved! But go check with 8A. The problem may be there now!"

"THE PROBLEM MAY BE THERE NOW!" the cry went up.

"Rose sent the problem to 8A!" a woman shouted. "Our troubles are over."

"The problem's in 8A! The problem's in 8A," people cried with relief and pleasure.

"What's 8A?" Blue asked above the tumult.

"It's an asteroid, idiot!" a man near him explained. "That's obvious. It's where Rose sent the problem!"

"No, it's not an asteroid," Rose objected. "It's an apartment with a couple of really old people . . ."

But no one listened to her small voice.

Someone started a chant:

"Our Rose! No snows! Our Rose! No snows!"

Rose felt very uncomfortable, not to mention very exposed, being held up on people's shoulders. "Please put me down," she said to Blue. "This is all wrong."

But her presence had put spirit and confidence into the crowd.

"Our Rose! No snows!" they continued to shout.

And even as Rose thought this, the eyes seemed to fade, and the street began to tremble as an earthquake shook the city. Then it stopped, and a slow snow began to fall.

"How does the Ice Queen know my name, Blue?" Rose asked from atop a Norkian man's shoulders.

"Louis and the SPASM can tell you that better than I can," Blue said. "C'mon. I'll take you to see them. I'm not afraid of the Ice Queen. My dad—" He looked sad and confused again when he mentioned his father. "My dad told me everything worth knowing about her."

The man finally let her down, and Blue took Rose by the hand and whistled loudly to hail a pigeon.

"Your dad sounds like a wise man," Rose said, as gently as she could. "Maybe we could get him into a shelter or something."

"No," Blue Boghen said. "He's in Central Park, you see. Near the Carousel. I can leave him food but . . . but of course I can't go *in* there."

Rose couldn't understand why he seemed so frightened of Central Park. "What's wrong with your Central Park?" she asked. "I practically live in ours."

Blue looked at her in shock. "You do?"

But before she could explain, a passenger pigeon landed beside them at last, blinked the snow out of its eyes, and they were off, aloft above U Nork, the crowd still chanting her name.

* * *

Rose was back in the control room of U Nork, with the dark-wood paneling and the thousand screens. Even though they were indoors, she could still feel the chill . . . and now and then there would be an ominous tremor, like that of a far-off earthquake.

The screens were filled with images of strange space-women, who seemed to be made of nebulae, each one made of thousands of tiny stars. Louis and the SPASM were at her elbow, and so was the young mayor, who looked, Rose thought frankly, in over his head. She had asked Blue to come inside with her, but he had refused, saying he had to get back to work.

"We didn't tell you everything, Rose," the SPASM said.

"We purposely let ya leave without knowing what Spot eats. . . ." Louis continued.

"Wait. You mean you knew Spot would get sick? You mean it *was part of a plan*? How could you?"

"Rose, we needed to be sure you'd return! We can't defeat the Ice Queen without you," Louis said.

"You ought to know—" the SPASM began.

"No!" Rose said firmly. "Feed my dog! Then talk."

"We'll have to go back to the diamond, then," the SPASM said.

And so moments later, Rose once again was descending on the elevator with Louis and the SPASM. She could hear little yappings of excitement as they descended.

They came to the doors, and then to the glowing diamond. Rose felt little Spot rooting and twisting in her pocket—and then to her shock, the dog leaped frantically out of her pocket toward the gleaming stone.

She caught him just as he was about to plummet down headfirst.

"It's all right," Louis said. "Norkies live on diamond dust. They were bred to eat it. It's a kind of medicine for them. Like gravel in the stomach of cows. They can't eat normal food unless their stomachs are lined with diamond dust."

Rose saw that a fine mist of diamond dust rose from the gem. She held out her hand. The diamond dust settled in it. She held it down, and Spot greedily began to lick it from her palm. He was instantly better.

Louis laughed. "That's a Norky for you!" he said.

Rose's heart rose as she saw Spot devouring the diamond dust. She even slipped some into her pockets to feed him when they got back to New York.

"Sorry not to have told ya," he said, looking sheepishly at Rose, "but we needed to be sure you'd come back to us, and you were such an obviously good dog-keeper that we knew nothin' could hold you back from feeding your puppy."

"I guess it's okay, Louis. I'm just happy he's all better."

She held out her hand for more dust, and then brought it down for Spot to eat. He leaped and barked with pleasure.

"Now, what else did you guys 'forget' to mention?" Rose asked. "Tell me the rest. Like, why does the Ice Queen know my name?"

Louis sighed. "See—the Ice Queen, her real name is Alma. And the truth is, well, the truth is that she knows everything that goes on here. She's from around here. She's a native of this burg!"

"From U Nork!" Rose said.

"She's half Norkian—and half Yorkian. See, she's the daughter of the Flying Visitor. And that's a combination that makes for some weird results."

"You mean the man from New York who planned the city?

"Yeah. That very guy. While helping us redesign the city, the Flying Visitor fell in love with a Norkian woman. Really beautiful she was, too. And we were all so grateful to him for helping us, it was only natural to encourage him to stay with us." Now the screens showed a picture of a gentle, beautiful heart-shaped woman's face. "He did, of course. And they had four children—daughters.

"But, like I said, Rose—something *very* strange happens when a New Yorker marries a Norkian. Their children were kind of, well, kind of divine," Louis added.

"Queens, they were," the SPASM picked up the tale. "Goddesses, almost. Shape-changers and star shifters. At moments they were as small as girls, at the next, as large as worlds. They were at home here in Nork, but free to travel. And travel they did, until they found four brothers. . . ."

The videos showed the four cosmic queens flirting with four constellation-shaped brothers. Their long, star-pointed bodies danced and twisted and intertwined.

"They found four brothers, from mixed-up parentage like theirs, who were cosmic, too. They had given themselves the names of the four spirits of life: Hearth, Home, Harp, and Hilarity—one for cooking, one for the household, one for music, and one for laughter. . . ."

Rose now saw four happy brothers assembled from stars: one built a fire, the next constructed a house, one strummed on a stringed instrument and sang, and the last seemed to laugh with glee at the others.

"And each sister married a brother, and the cities of the cosmos were, for a while, in harmony. Alma, the Ice Queen, lived with the Lord of the Hearth—ice and fire together—and they had a family. A small daughter. And they lived gaily together at the edge of the cosmos. But they always came home to U Nork.

"Then one wintry day, standing happily on the

corner of Avenue Five, a bad cosmic wind blew through the galaxy, and a splinter of diamond-ice entered Alma's eye."

"That happens in New York, too!" Rose said. She always got something in her eye when the subway came rushing by, kicking up dirt with its *floosh* of hot air. "Cinders and things get blown into people's eyes. It happened once to me. . . ." Her voice trailed away. She realized that it was a bit off-topic. But it was true.

"And once the diamond-dust was in her eye," the SPASM said, ignoring Rose, "her heart turned cold. From that time on, all she wanted was cold things: ice, and snow, and gems. And she came to hate U Nork, because we didn't want to turn the city to eternal winter, like she wanted. Even her father, the Flying Visitor, could no longer reach her, and in sadness he flew away from us, back in the silver zeppelin in which he had arrived. His wife went with him, too, and we haven't seen either of them since."

"The other sisters tried to cure the sick one. But Alma, the Ice Queen, turned colder and colder. Poor heart-broken Lord of the Hearth had no choice but to run away with their daughter to keep them safe. Alma was furious. She swore revenge on U Nork—swore that she would bring a new Ice Age to our city!—and she retreated to the fringes of the cosmos to plan her revenge."

As the SPASM spoke, Rose saw it all in the screens of

the control room—the vengeful mother, the distraught father, and the child swept away.

"So you see, Rose," Louis said. "It's not just the diamond. Oh, she wants the diamond. But she wants the end of the city even more. And she knows that only you can save us."

"But why me? Why does she think—"

"The three sisters made us one promise: that if ever the Ice Queen found our hiding place, someone even more powerful than her would appear in the skies and stars above U Nork—someone who the Ice Queen could never harm. And so when we saw you, we knew—"

Me! More powerful than the Ice Queen! Rose was staggered by the thought. Of all the people in the world . . . and then she understood what people who have to do something difficult and important all understand eventually: there isn't any justice or fairness in being asked to be a hero. It's just the job you're given. And, for some reason that she could not yet grasp, she was expected to save U Nork, and now she would have to do it.

She reached out her hand to feed her newly happy Norky. As she listened to Spot slurping up the dust of the enormous diamond, she wondered what on earth—or beneath it—she could possibly do.

* * *

Rose had to rush to get home before daybreak, so Louis led her toward the entrance to the steps.

But before making her way across, she hesitated. "Is there another gate between the two cities?" She told Louis about the wild dogs and the pink limousine. "If it's really true that I'm the one to save U Nork, I want to be sure I can come back."

Louis looked grave. "No, Rosie," he said, shaking his head. "The only other one—it's also in Central Park. But the steps across the water bring you here to the center of town. The gate beneath the lintel—the one in the Ramble— that takes you *into* Central Park, our Central Park. I don't wantcha *ever* goin' there, kiddo." He shook his head again.

Rose couldn't help but laugh. Louis looked so serious. "Louis, I practically *live* in Central Park. I'm not scared of it. You guys are just such city folk that even a park scares you. It's just trees and squirrels and dog poop and an occasional drunk, sad person. It doesn't scare me. You have to get out more."

Louis wrinkled his nose. "It ain't quite like that here, Rosie . . . It's—just don't do it. I'll travel back across the steps to get you if you need help. The Ice Queen's got her people everywhere. They're her zombies—get a speck of her ice in your eye, you become her slave."

Rose was getting ready to mount the steps when she

remembered the last question in her mind. "Louis, who's Blue Boghen's father?"

"You don't want to have anything to do with that character, Rosie!" Louis said quickly. "Or that kid of his either. They're bad news! Strictly."

Rose wanted to ask why Blue Boghen was bad news—she had liked him—but before she could speak, Louis had thrust her back across the steps. A moment later she found herself on the cold, damp grass of the Great Lawn. She tiptoed her way home through the early morning gray light of New York.

Rose slipped into her bedroom, yawning, and changed her clothes. Then she went into the kitchen. By now, her father was awake and reading the newspaper with his coffee. "Hey, Rosie," he said. "Weird news."

Rose was shocked when she saw the headline:

SENILE SCRIBE GOES BERSERK
DESTROYS OFFICE OF FASHION QUEEN!

Underneath was a blurred black-and-white picture, the kind you get from one of those video-surveillance cameras, of Joe Murphy with an evil leer on his face, holding an ax, caught in the ruins of Ultima Thule's office.

Chapter Eight

A REBUS

"Can you believe that?" her father asked, pointing to the headline. He was wearing pajamas and looked a little lame, as parents in pajamas always do. Parents in suits and dresses you can tolerate, but once they're in their nightwear, Rose thought, it was always a little hard to take.

Her father was frowning. "Joe must have gone *nuts*. I guess it got to him at last. The end of things, I mean, of books and bookstores and everything else he talks about. The trouble is that no one knows where he's gone. He's not in his apartment. Why would he have ripped up Ultima's office that way? You had lunch with him just yesterday, Rose. Was he upset about something?"

"Not really. No," Rose said, carefully.

"Where can he be? I hope he's okay. The police are searching for him, and so on . . ."

"Did he leave a note?"

"Doesn't seem to have. Here, you can read about it." Shaking his head sadly, her father tossed her the paper.

Rose read the article carefully. "Berserk writer . . . rumors . . . last published twenty-six years ago . . ."

Then there was a commentary about how writers put out of work by the Internet were going crazy. But Rose knew, deep down, that whatever was going on with Mr. Murphy, it had nothing to do with the Internet. It couldn't just be a coincidence that yesterday she found that dollhouse prison in Ultima's office, and now gentle old Joe Murphy had gone berserk and become a ransacker and had gone suddenly missing. Something terribly sinister seemed to be going on. She needed to find Mr. Murphy to find out the truth. But where could he have gone?

The only place she could even begin to search for him was at Medusa Books.

But even as she thought this, she heard heavy, clunking footsteps in the hall outside. Rose turned and saw their father was standing in the doorway. Beside him were two New York City policemen. They looked large, the way policemen always look because of all the things they have hanging on their belts: handcuffs and billy clubs and very ominous-looking pistols. Both these men had thin, skeptical mustaches.

Her father looked not just worried but frightened. For half a minute, she thought that Oliver must have downloaded an illegal file onto his computer, but then her father turned to her.

"Rose, these officers want to speak to you about something. Can you come into the living room?"

Her heart beat quickly as she followed them.

"Listen, Rose," one of the officers said. "Don't be afraid. You're not in any kind of trouble." He looked up at her father as he spoke. "We just heard that you had lunch yesterday with Mr. Murphy, and wondered if you could help us find out where he was." They had pictures of Mr. Murphy, and they wanted to know if he had said anything about Ultima.

Rose kept her cool and answered carefully. Her mother and father stood on either side of her, encouraging her to answer questions accurately, but glaring at the policemen, too, as though they might pounce on them if they said anything inappropriate.

Rose said, truthfully, that she didn't know where Mr. Murphy had gone, and that he hadn't said anything about planning to ransack anyone's office. Rose didn't mention the harsh things he had said about the world. And she didn't say a word about everything he'd said about small hidden hiding places in New York. Secretly, though, Rose was running his words through her head, replaying the conversation, trying desperately to recall all the places he had named.

The policemen listened, and though Rose thought that they were a little suspicious, she also sensed that they were just *professionally* suspicious. They were probably suspicious of everyone.

Only an hour ago she had been on the shoulders of all the people of U Nork, almost like their queen—with people shouting and reading her notepaper as though it were an inspired speech—and now here she was being, well, interrogated by the cops. It felt so strange. Which was she, really?

"I think she's answered enough questions," her father said protectively.

"Just one more thing, miss," the officer with the larger mustache said. He showed her something strange. It was a piece of paper, and on it were scribbled, in shaky hand-drawn lines, five symbols: a flower with large, over-lapping petals, an obelisk, the front face of a cube, and a semicircle; and then underneath, what looked like the profile of a coffee cup at the end. Above them all was a plus sign on the right, and a minus sign on the left. Like this:

She shrugged. "I don't know what it is. Where did you find it?" she asked casually. But the policemen only frowned, and asked again if she had any idea what it could mean.

"It might be a sort of symbol, like a signature—you know, a secret identity?"

"Like a tag for graffiti artists—you know, 'Lee' or 'A1' or something," Oliver volunteered. She looked up. Her brother had come into the living room and had been listening to everything that was said, and now stood beside her protectively. "Maybe it's his handle—flower, plinth, cube, half a round thing, coffee."

Rose looked at him gratefully. It was nice to have her brother pitching in to distract them. But actually, Rose didn't think it was a signature. She was sure it was a message. But what did it mean?

The policemen left their telephone number and gave her a long, opaque look before leaving, as though they suspected her of knowing more than she was saying. Then Rose went to Oliver's room to thank him.

Her brother was already back on his computer, as always, listening to music on his headphones. She could tell he was listening to Blur; the music was so loud she had to touch him on the shoulder twice to get his attention, then actually take the headphones from his ears to make him listen. For a moment Oliver was annoyed, but then he smiled at her, kissed her hard on her head, and then once on each cheek, as he always did, and Rose knew that she could always count on her brother.

"Thanks for before," she said quietly, and paused. "Oliver . . . I have something very serious to talk to you about."

"Okay, Rosie," he said. "I figured you did. It's not every day the cops come to give the third degree to your little sister."

Rose sighed. "It's complicated. And weird. Weird, complicated, and important."

She explained everything to Oliver, about the steps across the water, and U Nork, and Louis, and, well, the whole strange story.

Oliver didn't mock her, or make fun of her, or doubt her. He had once had his own strange adventure, of course, and that helped. But for once he took her seriously, perhaps because he knew that the world was a stranger place than it could seem.

So he said, simply: "Are you okay, Rose? If you are, then, okay, fine—show it to me. I think it's interesting that you've made that up, if you made it up. And if you didn't make it up, I'd love for you to take me there and show me."

Rose knew what she would have to do. Somehow she was not eager to show Spot to Oliver because, well, it was hard to explain. Spot was her secret. But, breathing hard, she reached into her pocket and took him out. If a tiny dog wouldn't convince her brother, nothing would. . . .

"Awesome, Rose. Look at that!" was all that Oliver said, and he reached out and stroked Spot gently. "So—show me the city," he said.

Rose breathed deeply in relief.

"What about school?" Rose asked.

"Come on, we'll tell Mom and Dad I'm taking you today. They'll like that." Oliver said.

"Okay, Oliver. Let me just take you to one place in

New York, and then I'll take you to U Nork." She faltered for a moment, though, remembering that the steps were being watched, and that she didn't know where the other gate was—the gate beneath the lintel—and Louis had seemed so set against her ever using it. But she would just have to figure that out when the time came.

"No idea," said the first of the three sisters as Rose showed her the sheet of paper.

As soon as the policemen had left, Rose had closed her eyes tight, and she and Oliver had copied the designs as precisely as they could from memory. Rose's parents agreed to let Oliver take her to school; then they ran to Medusa Books. Now the three bookish Cone sisters on the ground floor of the enormous bookstore had gathered around to look at it. They had been a little bit aloof the first time Rose had visited, but Rose sensed something else was wrong now. They seemed worried, even frightened, as she explained about Mr. Murphy's strange behavior and sudden disappearance.

"Maybe the smart thing is to see the last few books he bought here," the sister with the tortoiseshell glasses said. She went to one of the old card files, first sweeping off a pile of what looked like about fifteen dusty volumes from above it. She frowned as she searched through the little cards.

"Well, let's see. He bought a book on the history of the sleigh ride; a nineteenth-century pamphlet on the making of Santa Claus; a book on physics and nano-mechanics." She frowned at the mysterious phrase. "Oh—and he bought *Dr. Ally's Collection of Rebi*, a classic in the rebi field," she ended enthusiastically.

"What are rebi?" Rose asked puzzled.

"Rebuses," Oliver said. He had come with her to Medusa Books, but was off in a corner, playing with his iPhone. "It's a fancier word for the same thing. They're like riddles, written in symbols," he said, without looking up. "You know—a bee and then a U-turn sign, and a teacup, and glass with milk up to the top: bee-you-ti-full. Beautiful. People used to think that languages were like that. We studied it in school."

They stared all together at the five symbols.

"Obelisk, cube, circle . . . I'm not getting anything." Oliver sighed.

"You children had better go," Alexandra said. "Leave this with us, and we'll call you when we have some useful information." She said this very coldly, and Rose knew the sisters were not going to be any more helpful.

But Rose also didn't want to leave the sheet of paper, so she reached out to take it back. Alexandra drew it away, and Rose was about to protest when Oliver firmly shushed her and pulled her out of the store.

"You keep it," he called as they went through the door. "Call us if you think of anything."

"Oliver," Rose said angrily, when they were outside. "We needed that. You let her keep that paper?"

"No worries, my chubby companion," he said, reaching down to give her a gentle pinch. (It drove her crazy when he treated her younger than she was—but she had to admit that she kind of liked it, too.) "You think I didn't keep a copy?"

He reached into his pocket and showed Rose that he had snapped an image of the strange drawing with the camera of his iPhone. "Who knows?" he said. "Maybe the three of them have some kind of plan. Meanwhile, we can try to solve this for ourselves."

Rose's favorite thing to do when she was frustrated and confused was to eat something delicious—and it was her personal opinion that when you *weren't* frustrated and confused, it was still a good idea to eat something delicious.

"Oliver," she said, "could we go to Bloomingdale's and have a frozen yogurt?" Bloomingdale's, the great department store, was just around the corner and had the most delicious frozen yogurt in its eighth-floor restaurant. It always put her in a good mood.

Oliver liked this idea, too, and a few minutes later they were seated at the counter on the eighth floor, eating frozen yogurt on high stools above the checkerboard tile floor—right near the sheets and towels, where their mother always frowned over what she called "thread counts." Rose had rainbow sprinkles in her yogurt, while Oliver had his plain.

He spooned the yogurt into his mouth, still looking at the picture on his iPhone. "Actually, Rose, what if the plus-minus signs are the key? The ones above the symbols? There's a kind of cipher called a one-day cipher, where you have to interpret the message according to the signs that have been added to it. So maybe the plus and minus are, like, directions."

Rose crowded around to look more clearly at the image on the screen.

"Maybe they mean add and take away. Maybe each icon is missing something or has one extra thing. Let's take the first shape. That obelisk. Add something to it."

"Like what?" Rose said.

"I don't know. A color. A background. A name."

Rose stared. "A name . . . what name?" It was very frustrating for her. Ideas didn't always rush into her head. She tried straining out an idea but . . . nothing came.

She thought that it might be useful to take a few more

bites of frozen yogurt. "Well, if it's a name . . . then it could be . . ." But nothing came to her.

Eating her yogurt made Rose think of Blue Boghen and his kitchen. She wondered if they had frozen yogurt in U Nork. Maybe they didn't. She had seen no freezers in the open-air kitchen of the café. It would be fun to bring them some frozen yogurt. But how could she keep it from melting when she went across the steps . . . ?

Suddenly an idea, or at least an image, leaped into her head.

"Oliver!" she said. "What's the name of that tall Egyptian thing in Central Park? Near the museum and everything. You know."

"Cleopatra's Needle, do you mean?" Oliver said, rather slurpily, between bites.

"Yes! Cleopatra's Needle. That looks exactly like this first drawing. Maybe that's it—Cleopatra's Needle in Central Park!"

Oliver looked at her with surprised respect. "Well, maybe, Rose. Maybe. Okay. Hold that name. Cleopatra . . . Now look at the next shape. We plussed a name for the first one, so maybe we have to subtract something from the second one."

"You can't really take a name away from a cube. . . ." Rose said.

"Right . . ." Oliver nibbled thoughtfully on the end of his plastic spoon. "But you *can* take away a dimension! In two dimensions, a cube is just a . . . square. So maybe that's it! Square!"

"So we have Cleopatra, square . . ."

"Ah, I'm not sure about this, Rose," Oliver said, stirring the pools slowly forming in his yogurt.

"Let's just try the next one," she said. It felt pretty good to reassure her brother. Besides, she was sort of getting the hang of it. "A half circle, and we're supposed to add something to it. What if we . . . what if we add the other half of the circle to make it a full circle? Or maybe an O?"

"Yes, but in each case it's drawn with that, I don't know, brick inside—"

Rose suddenly felt as if her mind had been unlocked, flowing easily between images and memories. Rectangular blocks and that semicircular shape made her think of that experiment in science class last year when they learned about tension and compression. She learned you could make a bridge with a series of bricks if you arced it just right, and that the center block was called the keystone. And that that was also how arches were made. Arches! She flashed back to talking to Mr. Murphy about Arch Day at school. "What if it's an arch, Oliver? If you *added* bricks to the semicircle symbol, and imagined that the semicircle was, like, the blueprint for how to arrange those extra bricks, you'd make an arch out of bricks! Mr. Murphy and I talked about arches, so he knows I know all about them! He knows I'd get the clue!"

Oliver playfully knocked his little sister on the forehead for being so smart. "Okay, brainy. Cleopatra's . . . square . . . arch . . . Where does that get us? Well, *square* means straight and boring in old-fashioned slang. And *arch* means something that's too damn cute. So—cute and boring Cleopatra." He frowned. "That ring a big bell for you, Rosie?"

Rose was too distracted by the connections that her mind was making to answer. She could almost watch the links as they formed in her head.

"Maybe Cleopatra is where we went wrong," she said. She looked at the first sign again. "Look—it's *taller* than the others. So maybe what it shows is really a lot bigger than all the other things . . . Maybe it's . . . the obelisk in Egypt. Or maybe it's the Washington Monument!"

"Well, what does *that* get us? Washington. Square. Arch."

And they looked at each other, dumbfounded.

"That's where he is! The Washington Square Arch!" Rose exclaimed. She knew the Arch well, and the Square, too. Oliver had gone through a chess craze, and Rose had loyally gone with him on the subway to watch him play.

It had been thrilling, taking the subway alone with her brother in the winter, and then trying to keep warm by stamping her feet as she watched the chess players. Oliver mostly lost, but he won one game, and she was proud.

"Yeah! And the flower must mean 'Rose.' It's the, whudyacallit? The salutation."

"And the coffee cup!" Rose said. "Take away the cup and it's coffee. Another word for that is 'Joe'! So all together it says: 'Rose—Washington Square Arch, Joe.'"

"Well, what are we waiting for? Let's go!" Oliver said, banging down his yogurt cup with delight.

"One minute, Oliver," Rose said. "Let me finish this. Who knows when we'll have time for another snack?" She reached down into her pocket and felt for Spot as she finished her delicious cold treat. At least *he* was well fed now, too. As she stroked Spot, she dropped a few colored sprinkles into her pocket for him to play with.

"Listen, Oliver," she said, and she surprised herself by her own decisiveness. "Whatever happens, I *have* to take you to U Nork. So you go home and pack for us, and meet me in the Ramble around six. I'll be sure to get there on time. I'll go on to Washington Square myself. If we're right, Joe might be more comfortable seeing just me. He knows me, and trusts me."

"Rose—I can't let you go all the way downtown by yourself

on the subway! Mom and Dad would kill me if I did!"

"And the Ice Queen might kill my friends if you don't!"

Oliver was almost about to snicker at her, since her mentioning the Ice Queen sounded a bit ridiculous. But Rose looked so grave and serious as she said it that Oliver swallowed his laughter.

Rose thought she should reassure him again.

"Don't worry. If I'm late I'll call you on my cell," she said.

"You don't have a cell, Rose," Oliver protested.

"Uh, yes, I do," Rose said calmly. "I took Mom's." And she went back to finishing her frozen yogurt. She liked to eat the sprinkles one by one; but for once, she hurried her way through them.

The Washington Square Arch stood at the head of Washington Square in lower Manhattan, right at the very foot of Fifth Avenue. It was the gateway to Greenwich Village, which lay on either side of it—the pretty West Village to one side, and the funky East Village to the other.

The arch itself was covered with relief sculptures, kind of like paintings in three dimensions, of Washington and all the brave things he did to found the United States. Beneath the arch and all around it were benches and play-grounds and fountains. The chessboards were off in one corner of the square, with chess hustlers waiting to challenge the tourists to games, ten dollars a pop. The area near the arch was usually filled with mothers taking care of babies, gray-haired folksingers who'd been strumming their guitars for decades, and tourists who came to look at the folksingers. It was after three o'clock now, and children were beginning to walk through the square on their way home from school.

She had sort of expected to see Mr. Murphy, in his long coat and hat, waiting in the shadows beneath the arch. But there was no one. She walked around and around the arch, trying to see if there was any sign of him. He wasn't there.

But someone else was.

Eloise, her snow globe—loving frenemy!

What was she doing here? And why did Rose feel so glad to see her? She didn't really like Eloise—but Rose was lonely and cold and just feeling out of place, and in those moments you're often delighted to see people whom you know, even if they were never really friends and you never really liked them.

"Hey," Rose called out.

Eloise came up. "Hey, Rose. What are you doing here?"

"Well, um, nothing. What are you doing here?" It was as though Eloise were embarrassed that Rose had seen her. There was something weird about her. Her eyes had a dull, glassy look, as though she hadn't slept in days.

"I came down on the number six train," she said, a little flatly.

"You took the subway? By yourself?" Rose asked. That was weird. She couldn't imagine Eloise *ever* taking the subway, certainly not alone—she would take, like, eight taxicabs or a limo or something.

"I'm just meeting friends." Eloise had never exactly been warm with Rose, but now there was something cold about her. Not just cold—she seemed dull and listless, as though whatever she was saying she was repeating from a teleprompter somewhere off in the distance.

"Which friends?" Rose asked cautiously.

"Stormy. Wendy. Maybe you'd like to, you know, *chill* with us?" Eloise's eyes were hungry, Rose thought, but not in a happy way, and there was almost something scary in the way she said, "chill." Chilling together was supposed to be warm. But this sounded frosty.

From the west side of Washington Square, Rose saw two girls approaching. Rose waved, a little reluctantly. Eloise turned and peered out across the square.

At that very moment, Rose heard the sharp groan of an old hinge swinging open . . . and then a whispered voice called to her.

"Rosie! Quickly! In here!"

She spun around. There was Joe Murphy! Crouching down in a little doorway in the western side of the arch. She was so dumbfounded that for a moment she just gawked at him, shocked.

"Hurry!" he said, in his soft voice, beckoning her over. "While she's still not looking." Rose paused, to make sure Eloise's head was still turned, then raced over to the door. Rose crouched to go in. But just before Mr. Murphy could slam the door shut, she saw Eloise's head turn toward her and her blue eyes home in on the small opening.

"Too bad," Mr. Murphy said frowning. "She *saw*, I guess. Well, that's torn it. She'll probably get the rest and be back with them all within twenty minutes or so . . . well, twenty minutes can be as long as a century, if you use them right." He looked very worried, but then he remembered to be polite. He raised his hat. "Oh well. Glad to *see* you, Miss Rose!"

He was standing up now. The little door was shut, and Rose could see that it opened onto a stairway inside the arch. It was dark inside, and Mr. Murphy had only a flickering candle.

"You solved the rebus! I knew you would. Probably have Advanced Cryptography at that school of yours." He shook his head.

"Mr. Murphy," Rose said, out of breath with fear and

surprise, "everyone is worried sick about you! My dad is worried. The police are worse than worried! They're—"

"I knooow, Rose, I knooow," Mr. Murphy said soothingly. "Come up to my little home and we'll discuss it. I told you New York was full of hiding places. And this is one of the best."

"How did you know that message would—"

"Come on up, Rose, and I'll explain it all. We only have twenty minutes or so—but we do have twenty minutes!" He made a little gesture toward the stairs.

As they walked up the staircase by the flickering light, Rose could see that the inside walls of the arch were filled with graffiti and signatures that looked very old, as though people had been scratching their signatures inside the Washington Square Arch forever. There was no banister, and Rose had to struggle to keep her footing on the cold stone stairs.

At last they came to the top—a little room about the size of a small bedroom. Mr. Murphy had a mattress laid out inside it and a small electric lantern, the kind you see on construction sites with a guard around it, and a little Sterno can. A flag with a strange image on it leaned up against one wall.

There were cleaning implements there, too: brushes and brooms and small stepladders. There was no window, but there was, Rose saw, a little viewing slit in one face of the small stone room. The dim warm light of the autumn afternoon streamed through.

"Yes, Rosie," he chuckled, "I had to make my own breakfast this morning, doing some of my own cookin' right here at the top of the Washington Square Arch. Hidin' and waitin' makes a man peckish, as my good dad used to say when he was caught for hours in a duck blind down in Carolina. Of course, later on I suppose I'll sneak out to an all-night deli to order a sandwich and bring it back. But that presents its risks. It presents its risks! So a little Brunswick stew is just the thing," he said cheerfully. Rose thought how odd it was that Mr. Murphy always thought about his meals, even when he was in hiding.

"What's Brunswick stew?" Rose asked cautiously.

"Kind of a squirrel ragout!" Mr. Murphy said. And then, as though *that* was what was worrying her, he added: "Oh, don't worry about the facilities, Miss Rose. We've got a chamber pot and gravity operation going here, which doesn't *delight*, exactly, but does get the necessaries done." Rose wrinkled her nose, and he smiled.

"You see, Miss Rose, this room at the top of the arch is one of the best of the hiding places I was telling you about. I've been keeping it in reserve for a long time, you know. They made this space for storage when they built the arch, and yes, the stairs too, and then most everyone forgot about it. Then, a long time ago—a long, *long* time ago you would say—a couple of artist friends of mine declared it an independent country. Marcel Duchamp and Johnny Sloan were their names, and, why, they climbed up here and they flew their flag from the top of the arch, right up there"— he gestured upward—"and they declared Greenwich Village an independent country." He chuckled. "They held it as an independent country for—well, for almost four hours. Then the cops came, as the cops will, and they climbed down cheerfully enough. One key to the arch Duchamp and Sloan surrendered to the city fathers, as you might call 'em—the cops, I mean. And the other one? The other they gave to me, and I've been keeping it safe these long years, for an emergency. I ought to write about it, but I haven't, yet. Just as well. Kept it safe." He paused and gave her a significant look.

"But, Mr. Murphy," Rose said, "why did you come here? And why did you tear apart Ultima Thule's office?"

Joe Murphy laughed. "Well, Rose, I actually think that in this little story we're caught up in, I'm just a sup-portin' player, as you might say, while you're the real hero. Heroine, I should say. So—you tell me everything you know," he said, very seriously. "Or rather"—and his gentle eyes narrowed knowingly—"tell me everything I don't know—everything that you haven't been telling me since the last time we were together. And then I'll fill in the easy bits."

"Who were they, Mr. Murphy?" Rose asked. She wanted to gather her thoughts before she spoke, and one of the things that younger sisters learn is to ask a question to delay answering one.

"Who were who?"

"The artists. Your friends. Who came up here and made the arch a separate country?"

"Let's see. Weeeeeelllll, Marcel Duchamp, he was a Frenchman, you know, with a Frenchman's charming ways; an artist, really, who said that if he called a bicycle tire art, it was. And Johnny Sloan, why he was an artist of the streets, a man who knew the city and could paint elevated trains and late-night bars and bright lights on Broadway and all the other good big things we had in New York before the, uh, the reign of the tofites took over. That's their flag, the flag of the republic of Greenwich Village." He walked over and carefully unfurled the flag in the corner. It showed a knight from a chessboard against the skyline of the city. Rose liked it.

She swallowed hard. All the while, as he talked, even while she had pretended to be interested, she had been trying to decide how much to tell Mr. Murphy about U Nork and its difficulties. He might think she was crazy or that she was exaggerating . . . and anyway, the people in U Nork hadn't told her she *could* tell him. But finally, she just decided to tell her tale right through as honestly as she could. There comes a moment, she felt, when you have to trust someone besides your brother, and if she couldn't trust Mr. Murphy—well, then who could she trust? So she told him everything: about Ethan, or Louis, and the strange pink limousine that could run up buildings, and about U Nork, and the great towers, and the SPASM. And at last she told him her special suspicions.

"And I think, Joe," she concluded—she thought she ought to call him Joe by now—"I think that what the SPASM said about people who get a sliver of her ice or diamond in their eyes, I think it may have happened to someone from school."

Mr. Murphy merely looked out the little window of the secret room. He seemed lost in thought.

"I think you may have something there," he said slowly. "At least, in reference to that last proposition, to which I am becoming partial."

He summoned her over. Rose peered out of the little spy hole. Down on the ground of Washington Square, far below, was Eloise with Stormy and Wendy and all the other coolest girls from school. They had formed a ring around the arch pier that held the little door, and were all staring straight up—and though they were far down on the ground, Rose could see even from a distance that all of their eyes had the same cold gleam that Eloise's had. They shone almost like glittering ice.

Which was worse, Rose wondered, running from wild dogs, or from mean girls?

"Now, wait for it," Mr. Murphy whispered.

For what? Then she saw: two sweeping lights lit up the narrow streets around the square—and then the long, pink limousine swept by too, and drove right around the square, slowly, and around again, like an animal, a tiger or lion, circling its prey.

Rose swallowed, hard.

"Now what?" she asked.

"Now what, indeed. Of course, Rose, most of what you told me I already knew, or mostly knew." Joe held up a hand. "How did I know? That's a long and old story, which I ought to, well, write some day. Maybe I will when this is all over. But for the moment, all I got to say is that things are even worse than I imagined for your friends in our sister city. We gotta get you back to them."

He paused to consider. "Well, this is chess country, and I think the first rule of chess needs to be put to work here. Sacrifice the pawns to give the more powerful pieces freedom of action."

"Okay, I'll go down there and distract them—"

He chuckled. "No, no, Rosie—you gotta sacrifice the pawn"—he pointed at the woolen vest of his own suit—"to give the queen"—he gently touched her head—"freedom of action. While they're busy pulling me apart, or whatever it is your schoolmates are going to do, why then, you dash on out past them and get to Central Park with your brother." He bent down almost over her, and his usually gentle voice became urgent and rasping: "Get to U Nork. Tell them she's found out the secret—but she hasn't yet found where. Tell Louis. And tell them to free Chester. The time has come."

Rose had no idea what he meant. What secret? And where was "where"?

"Joe," she began, "I don't understand. Who should—"

But just then, from down below, a voice echoed from a megaphone.

"This is the New York City Police! Come out of there with your hands up!"

Both of them jumped at the sound.

"Well, Rose," Mr. Murphy said, "we'll have to bet that they don't have a dragnet for two. I'm going to climb up there and wave the flag of the free Village. Quick, give me your coat. And pass me that broom. That will keep their attention, all of it. If I'm not greeted with a volley of rifle fire or the like"—he smiled—"well, then they should be kept busy. Meanwhile, when you hear your name, you run out the little door and get to the gate. They'll think I'm crazy, which they do already—what was that word? Oh, yeah, 'senile scribe.' Okay, they could have said worse. Critics have. Remember, Rose—she knows *what*, but she doesn't know *where*, not yet."

Then Mr. Murphy took the flag of the free state of Greenwich Village, the broom, and Rose's coat after Rose removed Spot from the pocket. He poked open the little trapdoor in the roof of the Washington Square Arch and, sticking the flag through the opening, began to wave it. He pulled himself up after.

"Who dares to violate the free boundaries of the free state of Greenwich Village?" she heard him cry, as he clambered onto the parapet of the arch, waving the old flag.

It would have been embarrassing had he not seemed so serious and rather *noble*.

"My friend Queen Rose here is standing beside me in the declaration of independence," she heard him go on. And when he mentioned her name, she heard a rush of sound— "There! There!"—then the little room filled with the cold radiance of headlights from the pink limousine, radiating in through the small slit. And a cry from her classmates: "There she is! Up there! Beside him! There she is!"

That was her cue! She was supposed to run out the door! Gathering her courage, Rose clambered down the steps, shut her eyes tight, and threw open the little door. She just had time for a quick glance around—they had all left their stations and were pointing to the top of the arch. Then she ran for the safety of the far side of the square.

She was very cold without her coat, of course, and she looked over her shoulder as she ran.

Like a figure out of a dream, Mr. Murphy was high up on top of the Washington Square Arch, caught in the lights of the policemen's flashlights and the cross lights of the pink limousine, waving his flag, while a small figure stood upright beside him in a violet coat and wool hat—her! It was supposed to be her, anyway.

"Rose, here, won't take it!" he was proclaiming, straining his usually soft voice. "Miss Rose will defy you storm troopers of the mega-state!" He danced around the parapet of the arch with his strange flag, pointing with it at the purple-coated figure. With her coat wrapped around the broom and her hat on its top, it *did* look like her—from a distance, anyway.

Well, it was certainly a distraction. And a brave one, she thought as she scampered across the square as fast and as furtively as she could—like the mouse in their kitchen running from Rose's mother. As she ran, she heard a distant

gathering of sirens. It was as though there were two Roses—her, and this . . . *other* person who had been invented, who confronted Ice Queens and danced on monuments in New York.

"And then what happened?" Oliver asked.

"I don't know." Rose shrugged. "I guess they called the fire department to bring a truck with a ladder to get him down. All my 'friends' "—she made quotation marks in the air—"thought I was up there, too. They were jumping up and down and pointing."

"Weird. Nobody saw you? Did Mr. Murphy explain to you why he tore up Ultima Thule's office? "

Rose shook her head. "We didn't have time. But it was really quite a distraction. The way he was yelling and waving. It was like he was crazy." She wrinkled her nose.

"Maybe he *is* a little crazy," Oliver said.

"Maybe a little," Rose admitted. "Maybe having all that . . . knowledge bottled up inside you, all those keys in your pocket for so long, makes a man a little nuts. But it's a brave and loyal kind of crazy. It meant that no one was paying attention to anything going on down below, believe me."

Oliver looked around cautiously. They were standing outside the Children's Gate, the entrance to Central Park on Seventy-fifth Street and Fifth Avenue.

The autumn breeze was growing darker and brisker, turning into a sharp, almost wintery wind.

"Maybe we should call off this special trip of yours to New Oz, or whatever you call it," Oliver said.

"U *Nork*, Oliver. And no, we can't call it off. I have to tell them that she, the Ice Queen, has found out *what* but not *where*."

"Okay, if you say so, Rose." Oliver shrugged. "Now where?"

"It's somewhere in there," Rose said. "Somewhere in Central Park, Louis said. The lintel. In the Ramble. Oliver—what's a lintel?"

"A lintel's like . . . like a flat arch."

Together, Rose and Oliver walked through the shining mysterious lamplight into the dark, cold park. Central Park at night was lit by streetlights that bent gracefully. But as you got deep into the park, and deeper into the Ramble, the lights grew farther and farther apart, and their little pools of illumination became like a memory of a warmer world they'd left behind.

"The Ramble's like the mixed-up part of the park. They made it so that there would be a, you know, mysterious part. Not too grand," Oliver explained as they walked on.

"Oh," said Rose, as bravely as she could. She tried to rub away the goosebumps on her arms.

"Rosie, you're freezing. Here, take my jacket," Oliver said, and he actually took off his cool Sundance festival hoodie to give to his little sister.

"Thanks, Oliver," she said. "I love you."

"I love you, too, Miss Yummikins," he said, smiling. She didn't like being called that, but she liked the rest.

They walked and walked through the dark park, past the familiar play places where they had been so many times before. Rose felt so much safer being with her brother. They turned down all the winding paths and bypaths of the Ramble, until at last they found it: a gate with a straight plinth top.

It was at the bottom of a long hill, and stood just by a small stream which, Rose knew, went down toward the lake. An old-fashioned knotty pine fence separated the path from the stream, and the distant lights of the city fell on the lintel.

"This must be it," said Oliver. "Now what do you do, Rose? Click your ruby slippers?"

"No, no, you—you shut your eyes"—and she did—"and you sort of breathe deeply, and you wish your way across the opening. At least, that's what I've done. . . ."

She looked over and saw that Oliver still had one eye open.

In the distance came the sound of barking dogs. The lady in the pink limousine had found them. Rose trembled.

She had to get Oliver over before the dogs came.

"Oliver! You have to be . . . sincere. You have to believe. Do it very, very sincerely. And then—then it sort of happens."

She felt a tug, a firm pull, like a giant magnet, and she knew that she was on her way. She opened one eye quickly, to make sure that Oliver was coming along, too.

But he had his eyes open, and he shrugged.

"I don't know, Rose," he whispered. "Nothing's happening. . . ."

She could hear the dogs pawing the ground a hundred feet away, racing toward them with a deep, angry growl.

Suddenly she thought of something.

"Oliver," she said fiercely, "think of something you really, really want."

"Uh—like what?"

"Like a dog. Anything."

"New headphones?

"Fine! But think of them with all your heart. Really, *really* want them!"

And now Oliver shut his eyes tight. . . . Rose prayed that whatever he was wanting, he was wanting with all his heart. . . .

But still nothing! The dogs were only a step away now, and then they leaped.

Rose grabbed Oliver's hand, in fear.

And they were across.

She opened her eyes. It was still cold. And there were no lights on, which puzzled her. It looked as though they were in the same place. But something was different. The great towers lined the park, that was the same—but now she saw ragged firelight in the distance, not the gentle, beckoning lamps of their own Central Park. Just a harsh fluorescent light, hazy and all over. Rose's eyes grew accustomed to the darkness, and she saw that the brambles had been replaced with barbed wire and a high grim brick barrier stood where the little fence had been. There was a green metal sign on the barbed wire fence. Oliver flashed his lantern on it:

SIN-TRAIL PARK! WARNING:

YOUR TRAIL OF SINS HAS LED YOU HERE.

NO ONE LEAVES, ON PENALTY OF DEATH.

"YOU'RE IN THE PARK, OR OUT OF THE PARK"

As they read, they heard the sound of a baying pack of dogs. And in the dry creek bed they saw below them the glinting eyes of men in rags, gathered around a fire, looking up hungrily at the children.

With a sudden flash, Rose understood. It wasn't Central Park. It was Sin-Trail Park. And it wasn't a park at all. It was a prison. And they were in it.

Chapter Nine

THE GANGS OF U NORK

So that's why everyone in U Nork had been warning her not to go to their Central Park! She had heard them saying one thing, but really they had been saying something quite different.

It *looked* a little like Central Park. But it didn't feel like Central Park, Rose thought. A heavy aura of danger hung over the place, one she could *sense* better than *say*. She just felt it. A sharp bite of grim winter, like mustard or horse-radish, filled the air in place of the tang of late autumn that they had left in their own city. Dogs howled in the distance hungrily, not as though missing their masters but as if longing for a scrap of meat. And everywhere her eyes turned, as they grew accustomed to the dark, Rose saw faint lights. But they weren't comforting lights, like the streetlamps of Central Park. They were worrying, frightening lights: the short leaping flickers of ten or eleven ragged campfires off in the distance, and the harsh yellow-white haze of fluorescent lamps just over their heads.

"Hey, Rose," Oliver said, and he had a note of worry in his voice that she wasn't used to hearing. "What is this place you've brought us to? It's a little creepy . . . I thought you said it was great."

"It's the park in the middle of U Nork," Rose said. "See there, around the edge of the park—all those mile-high sky-scrapers? That's the part of the city I was telling you about."

Oliver placed his hand above his eyes to shield them from the glaring fluorescent lamps at the perimeter of the park. Then he looked at the high towers, with the tiny statues on their parapets, so much higher than the towers of New York.

Rose followed his gaze toward the outlines of the Nork-ian supway off in the distance, like a brightly lit dragon snaking its way in and out of the city. He seemed a little dumbfounded.

"Yeah, I see, Rose," he said at last. "Well, Toto, I guess we're not in Kansas anymore," he added, and Rose was glad to see his sense of humor returning.

"I don't think this park is like ours, Ollie. It's a prison camp or something," she whispered, as together they looked up at the ominous watchtowers lining the perimeter just above their heads. "That's why everyone kept telling me not to come here."

"Exactly, little miss," a man's voice behind them said. Rose jumped at the sound. "That's why they call it Sin-Trail Park. And why they generally recommend children to *avoid* it." The voice had a smooth, oily slither, and a high, sarcastic singsong sound. Rose turned around. Oliver put a hand in front of her.

A middle-aged man with long white hair, a double chin, and a look at once greedy and needy was watching them. He was wearing an old, worn coat, ragged pants and shoes, and on his head, a battered top hat. His evil eyes glinted like a jackal's in the yellow lamplight.

"How did you two get into the park?" he hissed. "You don't look like the type that the gentle Spaz would send here."

"We're, uh, just visiting," Oliver said. "And we'd be glad if you could show us the way out." He knew from living in New York that the best way to deal with someone menacing was not to show fear, but to treat them as though you trusted them and then to get far away.

"The way out! You want the way out!" The man laughed. His long white hair and selfish eyes seemed to be electrified by the thought.

"No. No, I think that it would be better if *you* showed

us the way out," he went on. Then he turned his back on Rose and Oliver and addressed someone they couldn't see. "In fact, it looks to me, boys, as though two delightful hostages have fallen into the hands of us Plug-Uglies, and they might show us the way out."

Rose looked past the man in the hat. Behind him was a row of even grimmer and shabbier men wearing top hats too. They were grinning nastily, imitating their leader, and Rose could see the edges of sharp and dirty teeth in the glint of the grim prison light.

"You're right, Lizard," one of the others hissed, stepping forward and drawing horribly close to Rose. He was fat, but not happy, Santa Claus fat. Instead, it was the kind of sallow, lardy fat you see on aging pigs. He had deep circles under his eyes and wattles that shook. "These two babies have wandered in? Then they might be made to wander *out* with some new friends they've made. Else the poor hungry Plug-Uglies might have to cut them and watch them bleed like little lambs . . . and roast them, too, over their poor cold campfire."

Rose shivered and tears forced their way to her eyes. What could she and Oliver do? The line of men grew closer. She reached into her dress pocket, where she felt Spot's tiny tongue lick her hand. She stroked him with her smallest finger.

"Yes, that's the way," the one who had been called Lizard said. "Tie them up and show them to the guards. And make them let us out. Or watch them struggle! Christmas has come early this year. . . ." They drew closer.

Oliver put his hand out again to protect Rose, but Rose could see that even Oliver would be helpless against these horrible and desperate men. Rose could feel their stinking and hot breath draw near, and see the glint of a knife—

"Get away from them," a new, deeper voice spoke, suddenly and sternly.

The Lizard turned sharply in the direction the voice had come from.

"What do *you* want, old man?" he asked, and Rose thought she heard a quaver of fear in his voice.

"I said to leave them alone, Lizard. You and Woolly and the other Plug-Uglies. The children are under *my* protection." The man who spoke stepped into the clearing near them. Rose could see that at the end of a leash he held a strong dog—a terrier like Spot, only this one fully grown. The dog growled when he saw the line of Plug-Uglies.

The man was small—quite short, really, she thought—but his posture was erect, and he walked calmly but firmly toward Rose and Oliver.

"I said to step away from them. They are under my protection. Food should be arriving shortly. Leave them

alone and all of you may have some," he added.

Lizard looked frustrated, and the fat man—he must be Woolly, Rose decided—sputtered and stammered.

"Why should we listen to you, old man?" he asked.

"Well, you could try to fight me, Woolly—all of you Plug-Uglies could," the man with the dog answered coolly. "But we've seen how *that* song ends. Or you could step away and go to the fence for the kitchen food. Your choice."

There was a long pause. Then, after issuing a train of spit landing inches from the man's feet, Lizard and Woolly spun on their heels, gesturing for the other scary men to follow. Saliva glimmered at the corners of their mouths.

"Thank you for the consideration," the deep-voiced man said softly. Then he turned toward the children.

"It's a dangerous thing, wandering in Sin-Trail Park at this time of night. How in Alstaire's name did you get in here?"

"We came in through the lintel . . . Louis told us about it," Rose started.

"Louis!" the old man said. "You really have been meeting with the elite!"

Rose couldn't tell if he was being sarcastic, or partly sarcastic and partly serious. But most of all she wanted to get someplace safer.

"Um, do you think we could step away from this

unpleasant place? To someplace warmer?" she asked as politely as she could. "And who, if you don't mind my asking, are you?"

The small, deep-voiced man laughed a quick, hard laugh. "Yes, I can see you're cold. And though there are no warm places here in this bad place, there are warm*er* ones. Follow me." He didn't tell them his name.

"U Nork is a beautiful city, but it is also a big city, and big cities produce small groups of criminals who tend to gang together. The people of U Nork had no idea what to do with them," the old man was explaining. It was about a half-hour later, and Rose and Oliver were huddled around a campfire in one of the meadows along with six or seven of the short man's followers, as grim-faced and ragged as he was, but without the air of menace about them that the Plug-Uglies had.

They all had big dogs, to Rose's surprise, and a string of horses moaned and munched just beyond the circle of men. They had given Rose a blanket, and what looked like a hot dog. The place wasn't exactly nice, but it was certainly nicer than where they had been. At least it was warmer, Rose thought.

"It began a generation or so ago," the old man went on. "The gangs of U Nork started as hardly more than groups of boys out for a good time. But then they became more ambitious—robbing stores, even banks—and then more violent: attacking riders on the supway, and even the mayor once.

"The people of our city are not cruel, but they would rather not solve a problem if they can put it out of sight. The traditional punishment for crime in U Nork was not prison, but transportation—"

"I know about that," Oliver said. "We studied it in school. It's when they send you away across the water to another country. The English used to send convicts for life to Australia."

"Well, in U Nork, the punishment was being sent across the steps to New York to drive a cab. That's why it's called transportation. They had to serve a sentence in transportation before they could come home."

Rose was astonished. So that explained why you never see the same taxi driver twice in New York! They're all U Norkers serving their sentences. And that also explained why they were usually so silent and quarrelsome. No wonder they're always grumpy, Rose thought. They couldn't wait to get home.

"Why didn't the drivers say so?" she asked.

"That would be the ultimate crime! Talking about U Nork to non–U Norkers is a capital offense. It could let the wrong people know about the city!" one of the old man's followers added. Rose was beginning to think of them as his lieutenants, since everything seemed so military.

"In any case, we couldn't transport all of the gangs. That wouldn't be fair to New York, our silent sister city. But we also couldn't leave them free to wander and rampage in U Nork. So city officials decided to take the old park, Central Park, which few any longer used—our people are not, well, not a people much given to a love of nature—"

"Louis doesn't even like looking at *trees*," Rose interjected.

"You know Louis?" The lieutenant laughed.

"He's an, uh, old friend," Rose said.

"As smart as he is short, and he's even shorter than me!" the old man said. Rose couldn't tell if he was being sarcastic or not. "So city officials decided to turn the old Central Park into a kind of camp, where the gangs would be free to roam and scrounge and fight each other and forage outside of U Nork proper. I say 'city officials!' At the time, no one was more part of that decision than I was. Who could have imagined . . ." His voice faded.

"We renamed it the Trail of Sins Center, which quickly became Sin-Trail Park, as you have seen. And then we tried to forget about it. As I said, kind people like cruel solutions as long as they don't have to see them. They were all transported here—the Plug-Uglies, the Dead Rabbits, the High Walkers—all of them. And they made this place their unpleasant home."

"Home sweet home," another of the men said bitterly.

"Yeah, but what are *you* doing here?" Oliver asked him.

The old man's expression settled grimly. "I had been the first permanent assistant sub-mayor, but I was sent here five years ago, after I had a—let's call it a *difference* with the SPASM."

"And a kangaroo court . . ." the lieutenant began bitterly. He reached his sausage out over the fire.

The old man cut him short. "U Nork is a mixed city. As I should know! It has flaws and faults. Flaws and faults aren't crimes and sins."

"What was the difference about?" Rose asked.

"That isn't important," he said. "But once I was in Sin-Trail—I won't say it was a good thing, exactly. Far from that. But it gave me a chance to see what life here was like and to try to make it better. Many members of the gangs were sickened by what their lives had become here. I gathered them near me, organized them, and taught them drills and discipline. And I taught them to care for animals. There is nothing so helpful for disorganized people as organizing the lives of creatures even wilder than they are." He shrugged. "If I am ever released, the gang members will have some hold on civilized life, and if I am not—well, at least I've brought a little light into this darkness."

One of the ragged men who had been caring for the horses approached them. "It's that time, sir," he said. "We had better get to the fence. Do you think that he's brought—"

"My son brings us all he can," the old man said quietly. "He's a good boy. We *had* better go to the fence. He's taking a great risk by coming here. We shouldn't be late."

They carefully doused the fire, and under cover of darkness, moved as one group. Someone scooped up Rose so that she wouldn't fall behind.

A terrible shadow had fallen on Rose's mind. "They don't *feed* you?" she asked, aghast. It was horribly upsetting for her to see this other side of U Nork, a side of ugliness and violence and unfairness. She needed to talk to Louis about it.

"Oh, they would never want the transported to starve," the lieutenant said. "But they assumed we could just forage for ourselves, picking berries and nuts, and trapping squirrels and wild pigeons."

Rose and Oliver flinched. Their father had once taken them foraging in Central Park, and it had been an extremely unpleasant experience, as they'd found only sticks and berries and leaves to eat. So when their father was busy foraging, Rose and Oliver had secretly sneaked out to a deli for greasy turkey sandwiches and chips. Adding a baby pigeon or two to the menu wouldn't have made it any more appetizing. Mr. Murphy might have liked it, though.

"There are even deer here, and wild boar. But we get desperately hungry for cooked food, prepared food—kitchen food as we call it. And so my boy Blue brings us what he can," said the old man.

"Blue!" Rose cried. "Blue Boghen?"

He looked at her squarely and intently. "How do you know my boy?"

"I met him on the street, by the cannons. You know, the food cannons. He said you lived here and that he, uh, steals food and brings it here for you. . . . But you're his—dad?" She was bewildered. She'd such a different image in her head of Blue Boghen's dad. More of a sad, homeless person in the park. Not this small military man.

The man laughed. "And I'm not exactly what you expected. Well, I suppose you can be trusted with my name." He stuck out his hand, a little pompously, Rose thought. "Boghen. General Chester Boghen. U Nork First Division. Retired, obviously. But not inactive."

He seemed to notice the look of surprise on Rose's face. He was a general? Could he be the one Joe Murphy had been talking about?

"Yes," Chester Boghen said shortly. "The ragged man you see on the other side of this hot dog was—well, I was the commanding general of Nork, and then U Nork, for—well, for a very long time."

Then he looked at her more carefully. "But you're Rose! Aren't you?" he asked suddenly. "Now, that's news!"

"I am," she faltered. "But how did you know? You've never seen *me* before. And if you're a Norkian general, how did you—"

"We've all seen you, Rose," he laughed. "We could hardly miss you. And as to what I'm doing here—well, that I can explain. But first, let's get away from here. We have a food drop to meet."

"Are we going to walk?" Oliver asked. "Isn't that dangerous? I mean, with those other weird guys loose?"

"No," laughed Chester Boghen as they approached the horses. "We're going to ride. Sled, actually." And Rose saw that behind the ring of horses was a row of sleighs—resembling the carriages you see outside Central Park in New York, with bored drivers wielding buggy whips and sad, tired horses. But these were painted a glossy black that gleamed even in the darkness. They looked, Rose thought, like military army sleighs. Even the horses had an alert, whinnying intensity.

Chester Boghen almost seemed to read her thoughts. "Yes, when they converted Sin-Trail Park from a playground to a prison they left a great deal behind. The old carriages and sleighs, for one thing. And the poor horses, too. For a long time they were neglected and ran wild, but when I arrived, we began to care for them. Now they can run like the wind and answer your call—just as the poor wild dogs who were left here are now as obedient as circus puppies." Rose felt poor Spot whimper a little in her pocket. She took him out gently to sit on her lap.

Together, she and Oliver were lifted into the backseat of the sleigh and a blanket wrapped around them. General Boghen got into the front seat and, with a flick of a whip, they were off.

It was still snowing, dimming the shining advertisements in the sky over U Nork, so that they looked like nebulae behind the clouds. Soon she and Oliver were skimming along, beautifully and silently.

There was something weird and familiar about it—as though she had done this or seen this sometime before in her life, even though she had never been sledding with Oliver in Central Park, and she certainly had never been sleigh-riding in U Nork before.

Then she realized: it was exactly like the scene in the snow globe she had broken. Rose and Oliver. The sled. Spot safe on her lap . . .

Of course, it wasn't perfect. They were in the middle of a sort of prison camp, after all. But it was *sort of* nice. And sort of nice is a good enough kind of nice, she thought, as she stroked Spot. Sometimes it's the best kind of nice.

In one way, Rose thought, it was just like walking through Central Park with her dad. All of the sections of Sin-Trail Park were just like the parts of Central Park she knew best. They whizzed by a carousel just like the one back home. But as they glided by, Rose saw through the clouds of snow that everything had changed: nothing hung from the carousel's framework. The carousel carriages had been ripped off, and the wooden horses leaned haphazardly against the surrounding trees. Men hunched over the horses and spoke to each other as they smoked cigarettes, while others crouched beneath and threw dice.

Holding on tight to her beautifully lacquered sleigh as they tipped down a hill, she suddenly realized what they had done. They had transformed the carousel carriages into sleighs!

In the Sheep Meadow a huge bonfire had been lit, and the convicts gathered around it, rubbing their hands with glee, roasting small animals on turning spits. Rose didn't even want to know what the animals were. Sinister men slipped back and forth in the trees as they walked, and Rose could hear dark murmuring all around her—but no one challenged General Boghen and his little band.

They came within sight of the fence that ran around the park. A single watchtower with a searchlight hovered above it. Chester Boghen held Rose's back with one hand while he raised the other high to signal to his men to slow and then stop their sleighs. Rose heard the horses sigh with relief at ending the rugged passage through the snow.

"The guards do their rounds at exactly ten thirty," he said. "Blue comes just as they leave. We only have five minutes."

They carefully got out of the sleigh and crept toward the fence. Nothing. Then suddenly, almost as though it were coming from the shadows on the ground, a boy's voice whispered, "Swordfish."

"Pesto," the old man answered. He grinned. Father and son gravely shook each other's fingers through the fence.

"Dad!" Blue said. "I brought as much as I could! There's some scraps of steak and bits of burger, and even a dozen unbroken eggs."

"Good boy . . ."

"But, Dad. You can't imagine who I saw—it was Rose."

His father laughed quietly. "I know. She's right here!" And he pointed to Rose, who was just over his shoulder.

Blue Boghen's eyebrows practically raised to the heavens. "What! What is she doing—?"

Just then a new voice leaped out of the trees behind them.

"You promised, Boghen! Remember your promise!" It was Lizard and Woolly; they seemed to be salivating as they approached, almost slithering along the grass. "Remember your promise, Boghen! You said that if we left the little pigs alone, we could have first pick of the kitchen food!"

Chester Boghen looked at them. The rest of the Plug-Uglies had gathered now and were standing in a grim semicircle at the edge of the fence.

"You promised, Boghen! You promised us first crack at the kitchen food if we left the little creeps alone."

General Boghen thought before he spoke.

"Get me a guard's uniform. But don't harm the guard when you get it! Then you can have *all* the kitchen food."

"All of it!" Lizard looked delighted. He peered around greedily.

"Remember: get me a guard's uniform. But don't harm him!" the general said.

Lizard and Woolly dashed away into the dark.

"General Boghen," Oliver said suddenly. He had been quiet for most of the past few minutes, absorbing the new world. "While the Plug-Uglies are distracted, can you please help us get out of here? Rose has got to find Louis and tell him what's happening,"

"Yes, please," Rose said. "Joe Murphy gave himself up to the police in Washington Square just so that I could get away and tell Louis that they must set you free—"

"Yes," General Boghen said, "I shall get you out. I have the outlines of a plan. But Blue," his father said heavily, turning back to the fence. "Oliver is right. When I was first imprisoned here, I was so disgusted with the rulers of our city that I swore never to leave until they demanded that I come back!" Rose thought that his eyes looked a little wild as he said this. "But now I shall swallow my pride—and go back to my city! The time has come! Rose and I both need to see the SPASM."

Blue looked puzzled. "The SPASM? Why? I thought you said you would *never*—under any circumstances—"

"I did say that. But there are new circumstances now." He looked up fearfully at the dark Norkian sky. "And now I need to apologize to him—and hope that he will help me. But, Blue . . ." Chester Boghen swallowed hard as he said the next words. "Blue, that means—that means that you need to stay here." And he quickly outlined a plan that would let him get away.

"Sure, Dad!" Blue said, after his father had finished.

"That's not a problem." But he bit his lip as he spoke. He was frightened—Rose could see that plain as day. And who could blame him, really! To be stuck in this horrible place, for who knew how long . . .

Oliver must have seen the look of fear on Blue's face too. "The only thing, General Boghen," Oliver said, "is that it won't work with just one guy. I'll stay, too."

"No, Oliver—" Rose said. But he just shushed her.

General Boghen looked at Oliver. And then looked through the bars at his son.

"Yes. I think that's wise," he said finally. "And I won't leave you here for long. I'll be sure of that."

Lizard and Woolly came back. They had between them a blue uniform: Lizard, the pants, and Woolly, the jacket. They handed both to Chester Boghen.

He looked at the uniform. "Well, it will be a bit tight. But good. Blue, give them the food." And Blue, very reluctantly, passed the bag full of stolen food to the two Plug-Uglies.

They fell on it ravenously, throwing bits and scraps to their followers, who leaped for them like sea lions in the Central Park Zoo back home, Rose thought.

"I guess that's what you get like after years of foraging for leaves," Oliver said. "They should open a McDonald's here or something."

"They don't have fast food in U Nork," Rose began to say, very knowledgeably, when she stopped. Chester Boghen, who had slipped on the blue guard's coat, turned to her.

"Rose," Chester said, sharply, "it's time. You must do it just the way I outlined. They'll recognize my voice."

Rose paused. A moment before, General Boghen had explained what he wanted her to do—but she still didn't want to do it, even though she knew she had to.

"Go ahead," Oliver encouraged her. "You're good at yelling and complaining." He smiled at her as he said it, but he did look a little nervous.

Boghen gave his son's hand a squeeze.

Rose took a deep breath. Of all the brave things she had been asked to do, this would be the hardest. Not because it was dangerous, but because it put someone she loved in danger.

"Go ahead," Oliver urged. "Call it out! Loud!"

Rose took another breath. And then, with all her might, she began to shout.

"Smugglers! Smugglers! I've caught them here. Smugglers!"

Nothing. Then, outside the fence, the wail of a siren began to sound, and within seconds, five guards dressed in blue uniforms with high, old-fashioned hats were opening the gate.

"Smugglers! And they've captured me! And I'm Rose!" she called, as General Boghen, in his ill-fitting uniform, winked at her.

The five guards raced inside the fence. "There!" she cried, pointing at Blue and Oliver. "One inside and one outside!"

The guards fell on the boys within seconds, pulling them far from the gate and sending them deeper into the park. The guards would have looked ridiculous had they not been so rough.

Witnessing this, Rose felt sure about her purpose. She knew what she had to do next.

"Quick," she said to General Boghen, addressing him as though he were one of the guards. "Take me to the SPASM! Don't let those smugglers go," she called back, though her heart shriveled, knowing that the smugglers were Oliver and Blue.

In the confusion, no one looked twice at General Boghen or thought he might be anything other than another guard. He held Rose firmly by the forearm, to make it look like he was accompanying her as much as following her orders.

Within seconds they were outside and running down one of the avenues, on their way to the SPASM.

Inside, Rose was sick with worry. She had brought her

brother to U Nork, never thinking it would be like this! She'd wanted to show him the sights and the people. She wanted to make him proud of her by showing how seriously everyone took her in this great city—and only *then* would they go to see Louis and the SPASM.

But now everything was dark, and she was frightened. What would happen to Oliver and Blue, now that they were captured in Sin-Trail Park?

General Boghen held her arm and pulled her along. Rose felt for Spot in her pocket, then bravely shook her head to clear it of all discouraging thoughts. She had work to do.

Chapter Ten

THE GREAT RULE

Joe Murphy was sitting in a cell in the municipal jail of the City of New York, desperately wishing that he had a book to read.

"That was a great, like, performance piece," a goth-ish girl in black clothes was saying to him mournfully. She had been in Washington Square, too, and had watched Joe Murphy wave his flag and scream out his rant—and she had been so excited by it that she'd begun to cry out too, and the police had arrested her right alongside Mr. Murphy.

Mr. Murphy smiled gratefully. But soon a goth-ish boy came to bail out the goth-ish girl, and Joe Murphy was alone.

A few moments later, though, he heard a loud argument rising from the sergeant's desk.

"He *has* to have bail. It's not a principle of what a judge wants or doesn't want that matters. It's the most fundamental principle of habeas corpus established in English common law. Either try him or free him!" the man was saying.

"He's an old man. You can't keep him here all night," a woman's voice added, trying to calm down the man as much as she was pleading with the sergeant.

Mr. Murphy recognized the voices of Mr. and Mrs. Parker, Oliver and Rose's mom and dad. He remembered what Rose had said about her father becoming very formal when he was mad. And of course he knew his colleague's voice. A few moments later, they were outside the cell. Mrs. Parker had long streaks of tears on her face. She was obviously worried about Rose, and she said so.

"Oh, Joe," she said. "Do you have any idea where Rose could be?"

"Now, don't you worry," Joe said, as kindly as he could through the bars of the cell. "They're *both* absolutely fine. They're with people who are taking the best possible care of them. Trust me."

But that only made things worse.

"*Both* of them! Oliver's with her?"

"Now, you just trust me, Mrs.—

"Trust you!" She'd been calm up to this point but now was becoming hysterical. "Where are they?"

"It's a little complicated. I can't really tell you where

they are, exactly. But I can tell you that they're safe." He thought for a moment. "And I can tell you who can help you get to them. If I could get out of here," he added helplessly, "I could even find 'em for you. I learned about that place a long time ago . . . It's sort of why I stopped writing. After seeing that city, I just couldn't see the point of writing about this one." His eyes went toward the ceiling. "But I wasn't allowed to write about that one."

"We've been trying to get you out, Joe," said Rose's father grimly. "But they say they have to run a battery of psychiatric tests on you first. . . ."

Joe Murphy smiled sadly. "Yeah. They're keeping me here because they think I'm crazy." He shook his head. "Isn't it funny how there are certain words they use and, it doesn't matter what they're sayin', you know it's bad? *Riddled*, for instance—if you're *riddled* with something—that's not good." He chuckled. "*Battery* is another one. When they say you need a test or two, maybe there's hope. But when you need a *battery* of tests . . . Well, then." He shook his head again. "I doubt I'm getting out of here. They tried tranquilizing me, but I managed to slip them under my tongue and spit them out." He showed the two slightly worn tranquilizer pills in his hand. "But if I can't *get* you where they are, at least I can direct you to some people who might be able to," he said, and he gave them the address of Medusa Books. "Now, don't you worry. Though I haven't had the honor of meeting Oliver, I know Miss Rose very well indeed, and I can tell you that what she's doing is something absolutely noble. Noble."

"You'd better be right," their mother sobbed.

As they turned to go away, he saw something in Mrs. Parker's bag.

"Uh, Mrs. Parker, I wonder if I happened to spy . . ."

She wiped her tears and looked at him a little suspiciously.

"I noticed you had, uh, that li'l book there in your purse and, as I have nothin' to read in here . . ." He gestured around his cell.

"It's just a . . . restaurant guide!" she said. "You can't go out to eat while you're locked up."

"No, of course I can't. But I can browse through it, and, well, it's better than food for me," he said.

"Oh," she said, and she gave him the small red book.

Mr. Murphy smiled as though she'd just given him the key to the city. "Of course, if you happen to hear rumors of hot corned beef floating around these halls, do send some in," he added, moving back to his bunk to read and wait. Rose's parents looked at him as if he might really be crazy after all.

Mr. Murphy's face creased from ear to ear.

* * *

The small man's long shadow fell suddenly across the SPASM's book as he turned the pages.

"Boghen!" the SPASM said. "How did you—"

General Boghen, towering above him, wasted no words. "The snow is falling. And the sky is cracked. You know what that means. Tell the girl and begin the plan. . . ."

"General Boghen," Louis's voice rose meekly. He'd been sitting alongside the SPASM in the high tower. He swallowed hard. "How did you get out?"

"I helped him," Rose said bravely, even though Louis shot her a dirty look as she did.

The SPASM seemed angry. "Rose! Why did you take up with this criminal!" he said. He looked at Chester suspiciously. "You're holding her hostage," he said, and he reached out to take her.

"I'm not a hostage," Rose said impatiently. "He is the man who—"

"This man is a criminal! Convicted by a court and sent to Sin-Trail Park!"

"This man," General Boghen replied furiously, striking his chest, "is a *patriot*, railroaded by the panicked!"

Rose felt frantic.

"You both love your city," she said. "You need to work together to save U Nork! Joe Murphy said that you should set Chester—I mean General Boghen—free!"

There was a long pause. Then Louis said, "He did? Did he, uh, say anything else?"

"Yes," Rose said firmly. "He said that she knows the secret—but she doesn't know where." Rose said this solemnly. And then she shrugged, as if to add, *Don't ask me!*

General Boghen leaned in toward Louis and the SPASM. "We've trusted other people's protection for too long. We never should have put ourselves in this position."

"General Boghen." The SPASM sighed, as though feeling a bit defeated. "We've been through this and over it. It's what your trial was about. You are not the only one trying to save U Nork. You need to listen—"

"I've listened long enough. Now you listen to me. We need to save the city by telling Rose the truth that only the few know. Tell her the truth, send her back, and let her *act.*"

The SPASM and Louis looked at each other.

"We can't *do* that, General Boghen. It is against the Basic Law of the City. It is a violation of the law we made when we left. I can't do it. You can't do it. It can't be done. You know that," the SPASM finished weakly.

General Boghen threw up his hands in despair. "Look!" he cried, staring out the window of the tall tower. Snow fell on the city and the sky above continued to crackle as if it had been short-circuited. Lightning struck in the darkness at broken angles, as though it were bouncing off against the sky itself.

"Tell her," said Chester Boghen brutally.

"It's against the law of the city to tell anyone," the SPASM retorted.

"It's a law *you* made, Spaz," General Boghen said. "How did you guys expect her to save the city if you couldn't tell her?"

Louis looked weakly at Rose. "We figured that she'd, sort of . . ."

He drew very close to Louis, who was just a bit shorter than the general was. "You figured that she'd, sort of!" General Boghen turned on his heel with disgust.

Louis glanced with concern at the lightning. "Spaz . . . that's never happened before. It's like—it's like the sky is broken." He looked worriedly at the old general and then turned to the SPASM. "General Boghen got put away for the good of the city. Now, I'm not so sure . . ." He looked again at the sky. "Maybe Boghen is right . . . Maybe we need him."

The SPASM ground his teeth. He was losing this battle. "But—" he began.

"But what? I'm sick of this old argument, Spaz." General Boghen looked up at the sky through the window. "If it is to all end now, at least I can end defending my city. We're not protecting anyone by hiding the truth. If we don't tell, we'll watch U Nork die."

The SPASM nodded weakly. "I heard you, Chester . . . I've always heard you. But we cannot change the constitution."

"Fine. That's absolutely ridiculous, but . . . fine. If we can't tell her, then show her! Show her! And go get my boy!" he added sharply, very much in command. "My boy is caught with Lizard in the wood. I want him out."

Louis sighed, turned to Rose, and drew the cigar from his mouth. "Rosie-toes," he said, "I think we gotta take one last trip on the steps across the water. . . ."

Oliver and Blue had run as fast as they could from the policemen when Rose and General Boghen had escaped from the park. But they had taken a wrong turn in the dark and, sure enough, run flat into the arms of Lizard and his crew. In the wilds of Sin-Trail Park, Oliver and Blue were caught in the hands of the Plug-Uglies.

"Boghen is out," Lizard said. "Boghen is out! The Park is ours to rule now."

"But that means no more kitchen food!" Woolly said, mournfully.

Lizard looked unhappy, as though he hadn't thought of that.

"We should let this boy go!" said one of his followers, pointing to Blue. "He's the one who brings the kitchen food. The bits and scraps are *so* delicious . . ."

"If we let this boy go, he will never come back. Can't you see that?" Lizard asked.

"But how will we get the kitchen food?"

This time Lizard didn't answer. He seemed to be thinking for a moment.

Then he said, triumphantly, "We must consult the beasts! We must watch the beasts dance and they will tell us!"

The Plug-Uglies were silent for a moment, and then exploded. "Yes! Yes, make the beasts dance."

Against the firelight, the men in top hats seemed rabid.

"What are they *talking* about?" Oliver asked Blue.

Blue shook his head grimly. "I don't know."

"Why do they all follow him, anyway?" Oliver asked.

Before Blue could answer, one of the Plug-Uglies holding his arm tight shouted into his ear in excitement.

"Because he makes the beasts dance!"

Before they quite knew what was happening, the two boys found themselves being marched through the park in the middle of the torch bearing mob. They were being led somewhere.

"The Clock!" The cry went up among the gang.

As Oliver looked around, he saw in the dark park ominous changes to things that in New York were normal and friendly. The statues that lined the Mall had been toppled, or had their heads chopped off and thrown aside, with mustaches and beards painted on them. The Bandshell, he could see, was inhabited by another gang, who looked at them balefully. Trash floated everywhere.

Oliver grew more weary as they marched through the park. Since everything in U Nork's strange Sin-Trail Park had begun as an imitation of Central Park, he thought he knew where they must be going.

At last they were in the place where the zoo in Central Park would have been. In the light of the torches, Oliver could see that the animals had long ago fled. The cages were open, and the pool for the seals and sea lions was drained, the cement on its bottom cracked.

But there, towering over it was a clock, just like the Delacorte Musical Clock Oliver and Rose had watched change the hours so many times before. It even had the same bronze statues of animals, dancing and playing instruments.

The Plug-Uglies took their places around the clock. Then Lizard disappeared behind the clock.

"Dance, beasts! Dance! And tell the truth!" he cried from the shadows.

Nothing. Then, suddenly, just as Lizard emerged, the tinkling music-box music began. He raised his arms dramatically, and his long hair shone in the light of the torches. The animals began to turn around their plinth, dancing and playing their instruments. The bear beat his drum; the lion blew on his kazoo; the kangaroo played a triangle.

Had he not been so cold and frightened, Oliver would have burst out laughing. They were just clockwork animals wound up by a custodian's key. It was all so ridiculous!

But then he saw the rapt, expectant faces of the Plug-Uglies in the torchlight, and he knew that for them it was not ridiculous at all. They were watching the dancing bronze animals as though they were gods, or prophets. Having spent years living in Sin-Trail Park, this heart of darkness in the middle of U Nork, they must have found the dancing animal clock the most glorious thing they'd seen in ages.

"Wherever they stop, the answer lies!" Lizard wheezed.

In the light of the torches, the animals turned and moved again. Even Oliver, who knew what they were and how they worked, was a little spooked by them.

"I feel it, I can hear him speaking. It is . . . the bear!"

Sure enough, the clock turned and wheeled and

stopped—and it was the bear who stood beneath the clock's hands.

"It's just a machine!" Oliver whispered to Blue.

"The bear says—feed on what you have!" Lizard cried in his rasping voice. "Make the prisoners your kitchen food!"

He turned toward them, his eyes alight, teeth gleaming, and his knife raised.

"The bear says so! Build a fire and eat the prisoners!"

Oliver gulped hard as the knife shone in the light of the artificial stars above. He glanced up: the stars, filled with their animated advertisements, seemed grotesque and nightmarish with Lizard's bright knife so near. Keep your head, Oliver thought to himself, please keep your head. He had one chance.

Quickly, he bolted from the Plug-Ugly who was holding him tight. But instead of running into the circle of armed men, he seized Lizard by the hands and began to dance a strange dance with him, raising his arms high and waltzing hysterically around.

"The beasts are dancing! The beasts are dancing!" Oliver cried.

Blue looked at him dubiously. But the mad dance continued. The Plug-Uglies watched in a kind of daze.

Then Lizard screamed, "Get him away from me! Get him off of me!"

Several of the Plug-Uglies at last raced over and pulled Oliver away. They threw Oliver back into a heap by the campfire alongside Blue.

He landed with a thud.

"Are you okay?" Blue whispered.

Oliver nodded. "I got the key," he answered back. "I did a watch steal. I practice on Rose all the time."

And before anyone could contain him, Oliver was on his feet.

"The magic is in me, too!" he cried. "Now, look! I can also make the animals dance."

There was a silence.

"No, he can't," Lizard cried. "No one can but me!" Then he saw that the key was missing from his wrist.

But the Plug-Uglies were transfixed by Oliver. Lizard, Blue realized, had convinced them so well that the clock was magic that now they paid more attention to the clock than to him!

"I, too, can make the animals dance!" Oliver repeated. He walked behind the clock, disappeared for a second, and then jumped out dramatically. He raised his arms theatrically, as he had seen Lizard do a moment before.

The animals began to dance and play, slowly turning on their base. How strange it was to hear their tinny, tinkling music in so dark a setting, Oliver thought, even as he watched.

Lizard simmered in rage.

Oliver raised his hands. "I hear kangaroo speaking!" he said. "He says—to let go of the food boy and allow him to approach."

The Plug-Uglies looked uneasily among themselves.

Lizard was almost beside himself with frustration. "No, no! Don't let him go!" he cried.

The Plug-Uglies, Blue could see, were torn: they believed in Lizard, but they also believed in the clock.

Rushing into their moment of indecision, Oliver grabbed Blue by the wrists and pulled him forward. He handed Blue the key and signaled to him to put it in his pocket.

"Kangaroo says," Oliver cried desperately, as though it were the silent animal and not Oliver who was making the decision. "Kangaroo says—let them go!"

The Plug-Uglies watched, torn.

The two boys began to run.

"Rose," said Louis. They had come back across the steps across the water. Louis had led her back, and though she thought she heard alarming noises when they passed over the grumble of angry, distant dogs—nothing had happened.

Now they were walking along Eighty-fifth Street, on their way to Rose's house. Louis insisted that he needed her to "see something," but Rose was just as insistent that she see her parents first.

Louis had put his Ethan-gear back on—a Jets T-shirt and synthetic pants—but still he had a cigar planted squarely in the center of his mouth. He looked half like a midget and half like a small Manhattan boy. It was very strange, Rose thought, to be walking the streets with him; but the truth was that no one on the streets really seemed to notice them. People in New York are used to anything, even U Norkers.

On their way to Rose's apartment building, they passed by the store where she had bought the two snow globes with Eloise. It seemed like a very long time ago.

"Hey," Louis said. "Do ya think we could stop in there for a sec so I can rest my legs, Rosie-toes?"

"Can't it wait, Louis? We have to find my parents—and we have get back to U Nork to save my brother and the city . . ." Not even snow globes could tempt Rose at this moment.

"I know, Rosie," said Louis. "But these bandy legs of mine get weary pretty quickly."

"We don't have time, Louis!" Rose said impatiently. "While you're resting, Oliver may be dying! Don't you care?"

"Of course I care! But a midget can't think when his

legs are aching. And a midget who can't think is no kinda midget at all. Give me five minutes, please," Louis said sweetly. "I'm a little guy, you know."

Rose looked at her watch. "Five minutes!" she declared. "Not a second more. This is urgent, Louis. It's your city that's going to be destroyed!"

They went inside. The store was as it had always been: the dusty shelves, and Madame Raines and her assistant. The old sofas, antique watches, and baseball cards. The man with long hair and the short-haired woman stirred uneasily in their seats as Rose and Louis came in, as if they keenly disliked customers.

Louis glanced around the store. "Look at these," he said, spotting a green-felt box under an old glass frame that had sixty different cigar bands from the turn of the century. "These are worth a fortune! You don't see these Lope de Vegas everywhere. It'd make a nice present for Doris!"

"Five minutes, Louis!" Rose said. "And does your wife smoke *cigars*?"

"Doris? Sure she does, Rosie-toes. . . ." said Louis.

Louis took the framed cigar bands over to the two watching shopkeepers and began asking them about its price, provenance—where it came from—and every other detail. For a moment, he stood between Rose and the watchers, and Rose felt tempted to do what she knew she shouldn't: open the tall glass cabinet and look at the antique snow globes. If they *had* to spend five minutes in here . . . the least she could do was look at something she liked.

As silently as she could, she opened the tall glass cabinet. No one seemed to notice! That was a blessing. She looked up at all the beautiful old snow globes, and her heart beat a little faster as she did. She pulled over the ladder to look higher, glancing nervously across the room as she climbed—but Louis seemed so excited about the cigar band collection that he had the two watchers equally involved.

From the highest shelf, Rose took down one of the snow globes. A whole city seemed to be inside it, and the snow was falling gently within, as though someone had shaken it not long ago. It had a big round building inside with a tall, thin, triangular one next to it. On the bottom was the label: NEW YORK WORLD'S FAIR 1939.

Rose put it back carefully on the shelf. Then she noticed another even larger snow globe behind it. She heard a sound as she reached for it—had someone gasped? She looked down from the ladder. No, the watchers were still watching, and Louis was still examining the cigar band case. She took the snow globe down and held it very cautiously in her hands.

This one was a real beauty. So detailed inside, and full of buildings and streets. It looked a bit like U Nork, actually. Even though she was still very worried about Oliver, it almost made Rose happy. The tall towers and the criss-crossing streets, even a billboard or two, blinking on and off—that must have taken real skill to make on so small a scale. She gave it the most gentle of shakes, and more snow started to fall.

As Rose held it carefully, she peered inside with an affectionate smile. It *really* did look like U Nork, with all those high towers—why there was even a set of statues high on one of the towers, just like at U Nork's City Hall. And there was another square that was as big as Square Times Square Squared. She peered closer: why, it was almost as though she could see people on the streets, tinier than ants, bustling along. She could almost imagine things like little cars running up the sides of . . .

Wait. Running up the sides?

Rose blinked.

Running up the sides!

She wasn't imagining it. There were little things moving inside! What were they? Flecks of snow, maybe, gone dark over time? No—they seemed to move in rows, in columns, in neatly ordered streams, like people on a river, or cars on a street. Some of the larger little flecks were racing up the sides of the buildings.

Then she saw the rectangle of a green park right in the center, and a stream of smoke rising from a bonfire. . . .

And at once Rose knew. She looked desperately down at Louis. He and the watchers were now standing at the very foot of the ladder, silently looking up at her, with sober faces that almost seemed ashamed.

She knew the secret.

U Nork was the city inside the snow globe.

Chapter Eleven

THE TERRIBLE TRUTH

U Nork wasn't at the center of the earth, or five miles high. It was right here. And she was holding it. The entire city of U Nork—its towers and its Sin-Trail Park and Square Times Square Squared—was inside this snow globe on East Eighty-fifth street.

She was so startled that she dropped it.

Fortunately, Louis rushed over as it fell from her hands and cushioned the snow globe beneath her.

"Hey, kiddo!" he said, half gasping and half laughing. "That would be a hell of a way for our town to go!"

Rose caught her breath. "Louis!" she said. "I'm right, aren't I? The city, U Nork, it—it's in there!" She was almost crying. It was so shocking.

Louis nodded grimly. "Yeah, kid. It's the big secret. Or the little one, I guess I should say. That's why I had to bring ya here—lure ya inside and all." He looked down.

"Louis, why didn't you tell me earlier?" She was so startled and upset that she was fighting back tears. "How could you lie to me?"

"Louis!" the old salesman in the store said suddenly. "You can't—"

"It's okay," said Louis. "She got down the snow globe, and she figured it all out for herself. Smart girl. I only asked her to come inside. So—it's legal. We can't tell anyone the truth about U Nork, but we can't keep 'em from finding out for themselves."

Rose remained on the ladder. Her head was spinning.

"But, Louis," she said, searching for words. A huge tear threatened to roll down her cheek. "You *told* me the true story. How U Nork was the diamond planet torn from a diamond sun. And how they brought the original citizens all this way, and how right in the center of the earth, upon the diamond, they made the tallest, biggest most beautiful city in the universe."

Now she really was crying. She loved U Nork, and she loved the idea that the biggest city in the world thought that she—Rose!—was a heroine. And now it turned out to be only a tiny toy city in an antique store on East Eighty-fifth Street . . .

"It *is* the most beautiful city in the universe," Louis said, and his voice had a gentleness that she had never heard before. "Just maybe not the *biggest*.

"See, Rose, we realized that if Alma was after us, we were *never* going to escape her. Her sisters, the other three queens—they knew it too, and since they were natives of Nork, they wanted to save the city just as much as we did. It was their hometown, too!

"But they knew that sooner or later she would find a way to destroy the city to get the diamond. And since we couldn't defend our city, we . . . well, we decided to hide. The three queens decided that even better than hiding beneath a world was hiding *inside* it. So, they put the whole planet into the sling at the end of the stars—it's sort of like a cosmic catapult, it makes big things small and small things big—and shrunk Nork down to the size of a . . . Well, they made it *this* size." He gestured toward the snow globe he held tenderly in his hands.

"And they brought the shrunk-down city to New York, and hid it away in the bookstore they opened— Medusa Books. They could live in either city, seein' as how they were the daughters of the Flying Visitor—being half Norkian, half Yorkian themselves, ya see. . . .

"And they left a few places in the little city for people to go back and forth between U Nork and New York, if we needed to—the steps across the water and the gate beneath the lintel. Some of us, we got star-diamond dust in our systems, which means we can change size between our city and the one outside. Your dog, a Norky—he doesn't even change size, always looks the same small size everywhere he goes, 'cause he lives on nothing but diamond dust."

Now Louis held up the snow globe lovingly and peered inside at the great city, its towers and parks and plazas and people, buzzing away beneath.

"They even took a part of the diamond and made it into a hard transparent shell to protect the city. So smart . . . so smart . . . Diamonds are the hardest substance there is, you know, Rosie." He knocked his fist against the snow globe shell lightly.

Rose could see that there was already a crack on the shell, and a hand flew to her mouth.

But Louis cooed. "The sky *is* cracked—but it's holdin' together! It's holdin' together, Rose—for now." He looked again at his city, and his voice was low and husky.

"So small! And yet . . . so *large*, small enough to fit inside a snow globe, but big enough to wow your mind! It's the biggest city in the world . . . and it's the smallest city in the world. Kinda amazin', isn't it, Rosie?"

By now Rose had come down to the base of the ladder. "But does everyone in the city know that they're tiny?"

"Are they? I mean, if they don't know it, then perhaps

they're not . . ." said the strange watcher.

But Louis shrugged. "I dunno, Rosie. Maybe that was a mistake. General Boghen thinks so, and maybe he's right. I dunno anymore. But at the time, all of us who were sort of responsible, we thought that it was too—well, kind of too demoralizing and scary to be told that you were being protected by being shrunk down to one thousandth of your old size.

"So me and General Boghen—he was a very young man, then—and the Spaz, we knew what was happening. But most people didn't. We put them into suspended animation—sort of like a long sleep—and when they woke up in U Nork again, well, we told them that the city had been rebuilt full size and all in the middle of your planet."

"And the Ice Queen? What does she know?" Rose asked.

"See, for a long time the Ice Queen didn't realize what we'd done either. As far as Alma knew, our planet had simply vanished from the night sky. Her sisters told her it had exploded like a supernova star.

"But then she heard rumors, and whispers, and at last she found out! She came to New York in search of it. Since she's half Norkian, and half Yorkian, too, like her sisters, she can live in either world equally well. And she put out word, over and over planet Earth, until at last her gaze fell upon this city.

"She came to New York and took the name Ultima Thule, which means the farthest northern extreme."

"Ultima Thule! She's the Ice Queen! She's Alma—I mean, I knew she was sort of scary but—"

"Yeah—it's her. It's her, all right. But just when she found out, about ten years ago—why, that's when *you* appeared in New York, too, Rosie. That's when we started sendin' the midgets to the classrooms, lookin' for you. Once they knew that she was in New York, the other three sisters knew they'd better not leave the snow globe at the bookstore—that would be the first place that she would look. So they hid it here. And then, of course, she found it, just recently and all—but you found it too, and we all took heart! And since it happened just after Ultima peered in, why, we figured you were coming to rescue us just after she threatened us! That's why everyone was so excited to see you. Of course, we'd been expecting you a long time—"

"Expecting me? But how—"

Louis didn't seem to hear her.

"Then the other night she came back in, and before the watchers awoke, she struck the city's shell with her stick—see, you can see the mark across it. Fortunately, the diamond shell was too hard even for her to break! That's what's made the storm in U Nork . . . But she would break it completely to get the diamond!"

Louis shuddered; it was terrible enough for Rose to hear all this, but for Louis, it must've been as if his entire world could come crashing to an end in a single moment.

"But *why* were you looking for me? Why am I—"

"Why? Because you got diamond dust in your blood, too, kiddo! You always have. That's why your brother could pass over just by holding your hand. And that's why you're safe. That's why we've been expecting you. See, she, the Ice Queen, won't touch you. She—"

"No, she won't. But she will touch you, little man," a cool voice said.

It was Ultima Thule. She was standing in the front door. Rose could see the pink limousine on the street behind her. Behind Ultima were Rose's classmates, Eloise, Wendy, and Stormy. They were looking adoringly, but unsmilingly, at Ultima.

How beautiful Ultima looked! Rose thought weakly. Dazzling, really. She was wrapped in white furs—not a coat, but some kind of floor-length wrap that clung to her long, fine form. The white fur seemed to glimmer as she moved, as though tiny stars were sprinkled throughout it. On her head she wore a silver fur hat of the same shimmering make. At her throat and on her wrists she had diamond bracelets, which glowed as though they were lit from within, and on the lobes of her ears were giant dangling diamond earrings. She was magnificent, Rose thought . . .

Then Ultima took out her BlackBerry and pointed it at Louis.

Two tiny pellets of ice shot out of its end. Rose could almost see the little ice slivers as it passed through the BlackBerry and struck Louis in the eye.

"Oh, no!" Rose cried.

Twice more, the BlackBerry spat, and the two watchers were frozen as well.

"Take the globe; leave the midget. And bring along your friend," Ultima said, almost casually, to Rose's frosty classmates.

"Never," said Rose, and she ran to the globe. "Louis!" she cried. "Help me! Save your city!"

But Louis only looked at her sheepishly and shrugged. He stared at Ultima, as though some dim memory of her evil remained in the recesses of his mind—but then his shoulders collapsed, and he stared down helplessly at the floor.

"Whoever is struck with a chip of the diamond is the slave of the first person they see after it happens. Which happens, as it happens, to always be me! Good to have diamond dust in your veins. Very bad to have it in your eye," Ultima explained slowly.

"Take her!" Ultima repeated, more brusquely. "I'll take this," she said, picking up the snow globe and its precious cargo as though it were just any another bauble on the shelf. Rose's classmates laid their cold hands on her and started pulling her out of the store. Rose furiously struggled and kicked.

"Let me go!" she cried, trying to wrest herself from their grasp.

"Madame," Eloise said, in a tinny monotone, "can't you—you know—ice her? Please?"

"No, my dear. Not her. I have . . . other plans for her. Plans that demand her being, shall we say, alive. And aware." She smiled at Rose.

In a moment, Rose was bundled into the pink limousine waiting outside, as Louis and the two watchers looked on listlessly.

Eloise, Wendy, and Stormy held Rose's hands and arms tightly down as they pushed her into the backseat. Ultima Thule got into the seat in front of her. She held the snow globe, and with a whole living city inside, gave it a shake, at arm's length, as though teasing Rose. Then she drew it back, burying it deep within her long and beautiful white fur wrap, which seemed to glow all the brighter with the snow globe inside it, as though it were a fire pressed to her icy heart.

Chapter Twelve

THE FINAL BATTLE

It was a few hours later, and Rose was inside Ultima Thule's office at her father's building. No one tied her up, or put handcuffs on her, or even did anything remotely like that, which was worse, in a way. Her classmates just led her to the big chair in Ultima's office and stood around it like somber guardians, their cold, unflinching eyes watching her.

What made it so maddening was that the snow globe, with U Nork inside it—and her brother Oliver, and her brave new friend Blue!—was sitting right on Ultima's desk, amid the other snow globes, as though it were simply one more bauble, and not a living thing.

And what made it desperately bad was that beside the snow globe, on the desk, was a hammer. Blunt and heavy, with its head turned down toward the desk.

"Listen," Rose said to Eloise. "You don't know what you're doing. That snow globe—it has a city inside it. With real people, tiny people, but real, and if you or Ultima smash it you'll be"—her voice faltered—"you'll be killing real people!" She was almost weeping.

But Eloise, her eyes dazzling and icy, merely looked past her. It was no use, Rose knew: she was the slave of Ultima Thule, the Ice Queen, and there was no hope. . . .

"Yes, you're right. There is no hope, Rose." It was Ultima, who had come back into the office. She was wearing a Chanel suit, black and white checked, and she seemed almost weary. She leaned back in her black leather chair.

"I shall give one last warning to the elite of the city to abandon it and hand over the jewel that they stole from me. They can then take up residence in my welcoming little villa—which you discovered so cleverly the other day—or else . . ." She smiled sinisterly, then picked up the hammer. "Or else—" She let the hammer drop from her limp wrist.

"No! No! You can't do that!"

"Oh, but it's already done! Can't you see? I took one small blow with my ring, and look—the city is already cracking." She pointed to the top of the snow globe, where the break radiated out little spidery veins.

"It's only a matter of time, you see, Rose. I had not known that the city's shell was made of the city's diamond!

Very clever, but as you see, I have the thing to shatter it!"
And now she held the hammer up so that its face showed
to Rose. Then Rose saw that the hammer's face itself was
made of diamonds, glittering coldly.

"Only diamond can break diamond—only the hard can
crack the hard! And now I shall get my own great diamond
back!"

"They didn't steal it from you—they didn't!"

"They did! *I* am Queen of Ice! The diamond belongs to
me! Had they just handed it over, I never would have lost
my child! They said that I had lost my way, and my mind—
and they took the princess!" She had a look in her eye that
was half hurt and half crazy. "She would never have been
lost to me if the Norkians had just given me the diamond.
All they had to do was give me the diamond!"

In rage, she picked up her BlackBerry, pointed it down,
and set it off again. Two tiny poisonous diamond pellets
struck the desk, leaving tiny craters.

Rose realized that, like all selfish and hate-filled people, Ultima had convinced herself that other people were
to blame for making her selfish and hate-filled. And like
all cruel people, she was also easily full of self-pity. It didn't
matter to her, Rose thought, that they couldn't surrender
the diamond without losing their city.

"All I wanted was the diamond that was mine," Ultima

said, and Rose could see that she was on the brink of tears. "All I wanted was the diamond that was mine. And then I lost my daughter. . . ."

Something inside Rose was touched by Ultima's loneliness. When she cried for her lost child, it sounded like a real feeling.

"You won't get your daughter back by destroying U Nork," Rose said, as gently as she could. "The diamond won't bring your daughter back. . . ."

"That's why you're going to be the one to tell them!" Ultima said with a triumphant air. "Tell them to surrender—or watch your city crumble and your brother die!" she hissed. "There's no way he can leave the city now! The gates are watched, and closed."

Rose drew a deep breath. And then an idea occurred to her.

"I'll speak to them," she said. "But—I can't find the words. Let me write down what I have to say. I'm not good at show-and-tell. Give me a piece of paper, I can't tell them to surrender. I—I need to write it down first."

"Very well," said Ultima.

Rose tore a page from the legal pad that Ultima had thrust at her. She set down to write—and she wrote in a slow, even hand.

"I'll tell them that the only thing in the whole world that

they can do is to surrender," she said, speaking as quickly and nervously as she could, hoping to draw Ultima's attention to her voice and away from her hand writing on the page. "I'll tell them it's super important for them to surrender right away and just give up. . . ."

And as she prattled on, engaging Ultima's eyes, at the very bottom corner of the paper she scribbled three little signs.

Then she reached into her pocket. Yes; good little Spot was there still. Oh, if only he had the sense to know what she had in mind! And if only Oliver and General Boghen would understand! And if only Blue was right . . .

Rose went to the globe while Ultima stood triumphantly beside her, and began to speak.

Don't believe me, she prayed, even as she spoke. *Please don't believe me.* Her fingers, just as Oliver had taught her, folded over the far tiny edge of paper, and tore it clean. Then, sweeping her hair back to distract Ultima, she snaked her right hand out to cover the little poison-pellet on the desk.

Now if she could only remember what Oliver had tried to teach her about the Mercury fold when he had been doing magic tricks. Work with your last two fingers. That's right—slip it under Spot's collar, and now bring him up . . . the diamond chip that clung to her little finger, and now, insert that too—and then before Ultima could see, as she bent over the globe, speaking those horrible words, she slipped the tiny dog inside the widening crack of the snow globe. . . .

In U Nork, at that moment, the city was in panic. The sky was dark, and the shaking that they had undergone was, to the people within, like an earthquake.

The whole town shook. The great avenues buckled. In Square Times Square Squared, electric signs came loose from their moorings and hung, horribly, by one side, sparks spewing from their cut wires. The well-dressed people of U Nork huddled in their apartments and cowered beneath their cars.

Then suddenly, from down below, the people of U Nork saw Rose's face, and everything stopped. Rose's face filled the sky, and for a moment everyone's heart filled with hope.

"Rose! Rose!" they cried.

But as they heard her words, their faces first turned blank, then filled with dismay. What was she saying?

"You must . . . surrender the city . . . everyone come out and march in single file. Safe beds await you." Then Rose leaned over and pressed her hands against the sky, as though imploring the people of U Nork to listen to her, to surrender the city.

From the high tower where General Boghen and the SPASM watched, they too saw Rose's face. Her words filled them with horror.

"How could Rose have betrayed us?" the SPASM said.

General Boghen had a telescope pressed to his eye as he watched the girl's face filling the sky. And then his gaze widened, to take in the darkness around her.

"Perhaps she hasn't. What was that?" he looked again. "I thought I saw something. Something's falling . . . it seems to me . . . that perhaps she hasn't. Quick! Now! Send every passenger pigeon in the city into the clouds, high as they can go!"

Down, down little Spot fell through the snow, falling and falling. *Wheee!* Spot barked and howled with pleasure as he fell, until he looked down and saw the spires and tops of the buildings rising to meet him. That was scary! Why had Rose dropped him? With a small howl of wonder and worry, he realized that he was really falling now.

But even as he did, the flocks of passenger pigeons wheeled and turned beneath him, forming a gray-black mass below, like a flying, soaring net. And Spot soon landed, plumply, right on the back of one of them.

"Okay, Mac," the pigeon said, pointing its nose a little

disdainfully at all the other pigeons. "Where to?"

But little Spot only barked. And the pigeon turned, and lowering his brow, swooped straight down, dove straight down, down toward the snowy city.

The Spaz and General Boghen were not the only ones to see Spot fall to earth on the back of a passenger pigeon. Hidden in the dark street just outside Sin-Trail Park, still out of breath from running away from the Clock and the Plug-Uglies, Blue and Oliver were watching, too. Oliver's quick eye caught the fall of something—no bigger than a speck of dust, it seemed, but he was sure that he had seen it: a little dog on the back of the pigeon.

"It's Rose's little dog!" he cried. "I'm sure of it. But why would she send Spot down here? Something must've happened, Blue. We need to find your father. Could we run to where he is?"

"Too far," Blue said. "We'll have to take the supway."

"The subway? Is it still running?" Oliver asked.

"No, the *sup*way. We call it that because you can have supper on it—if you can hold onto your food. It's automatic, so I imagine it's still running."

The two boys ran from the park toward the supway station, and were panting when they got there. Only moments before they had scaled the fence after escaping from the Plug-Uglies. The guards to Sin-Trail Park, like everyone else in U Nork, had been staring at the sky and its strange events when the two boys had come to the edge of the park.

A supway car pulled up to the platform, but the doors wouldn't open.

And then they saw him, clinging to the side of the seats. Inside the supway car—Lizard! He must have followed them, and escaped from the park when the guards panicked, too. He wanted the key to the clock, of course. His power flowed from it.

"Blue, what do we do?" Oliver asked.

"Quick, up here!" Blue called, and using the practice he'd gained from all those years smuggling food into Sin-Trail Park, he quickly scrambled up and pulled Oliver up alongside him to the top of the car.

With a lurch and a cough, the supway train began to move. Slowly it picked up speed. Oliver clung to the top of the car.

But Blue, using all the balance he had acquired, soon found his feet, and Oliver looked at him, deciding that he had better get up, too. He had his honor to protect.

Slowly and shakily, he got to his feet. Oliver had never ridden on top of a train before. As the train lurched and hitched he felt more nervous. But then he found his legs and almost started to enjoy the ride. As the supway swooped and growled through the streets of U Nork, it flashed past glowing windows and Oliver glimpsed families sitting down to dinner. Running within feet of cornices and streetlamps, the train made sharp, sudden turns between tall buildings, like a great dragon racing at bird's-eye view throughout the city.

"Hold on tight!" Blue cried, and Oliver grabbed the handrail running along the top of the car. It must've been put there for the men who maintained the line, he thought.

Slowly, the supway began to inch up a steep incline.

"Hold on *really* tight," Blue warned Oliver.

The supway came to the top of the incline.

And then, with a sickening, sudden drop, the supway fell vertically down the rail on the other side.

It was faster than any roller coaster Oliver had ever been on. He yelled, and held as tight as he could to the little handrail on top of the car.

The supway swooped through the streets and past windows and offices. It seemed to turn on its side as it went right by. It raced through a crowded neighborhood, and Blue, who seemed to be enjoying the excitement, reached for a clothesline and grabbed a bedsheet, which he held out like a sail, a big smile on his face as it fluttered in the wind.

Then suddenly, Oliver was aware of another presence.

He turned his head in the rushing wind—and saw two evil eyes glaring at him. It was Lizard! He had crawled up the side of the supway car and was staring at Oliver greedily; you could just see his eyes peeking out over the side of the car.

The supway car plunged and swooped through the U Nork night as Lizard—a knife between his teeth—vaulted ever closer to Oliver, in sudden leaps and bounds.

The train tore, faster and faster, through the city. On its side, around the edge of the Supernatural History Museum, so close that Oliver could have touched the Loch Ness Monster skeleton on its façade, had he dared to let go of the handle he had found! Sickeningly downward, straight down, on Broadway! Tearing through the blinding lights of Square Times Square Squared—and all the time Lizard was coming closer and closer, the knife set between his grimy teeth glinting bright orange in the reflections of the signs.

Just give him the key, Oliver thought. I'll throw it to him. But when he reached into his pocket, it wasn't there. He had given it to Blue!

Suddenly, Oliver felt a flutter of wind in his face, different from the whooshing of the wind from the supway's movement. And he heard a sound, a kind of flutter and coo, at once oddly familiar. He looked up quickly. Pigeons!

The giant pigeons were flocking around the speeding supway car. Wheeling and turning in the night air above them. And, could it be—yes! It was hard to see—he was so small!—but if he squinted his eyes, Oliver could just make out Rose's tiny dog Spot, gloriously riding between one pigeon's wings, clinging to its reins with his teeth.

It occurred to Oliver that they were trying to save the boys. As the supway car headed up another steep incline, the great birds circled beneath the train. Sure-footed and courageous, Blue got to his feet and, to Oliver's amazement, leaped from the roof of the car onto the gray back of a passenger pigeon. For one horrible moment he seemed to slip away down the bird's body. But then he grabbed hold of the bridle and steadied himself, and was riding sure. With a wave and a smile he gestured to Oliver to jump, too.

But Oliver remained locked in place, terrified. He could see so clearly how close Blue had come to falling. What if he tried to make the leap and failed?

Lizard had the knife in his hand now, and was looking at the frightened boy, ready to throw it directly at his heart.

Oliver shut his eyes tight in terror. Then he heard a loud sound, like a high cooing shriek, from the pigeons. He could hear their wings fluttering desperately hard, as though in fear.

Then, suddenly, he felt his body in the grip of a firm, locking embrace. He was being lifted from the roof of the supway car as it raced through U Nork. He hardly dared open his eyes, but the firm, crushing embrace, which almost squeezed the air out of him, was stronger than ever, and he could feel himself being pulled, upward and upward.

Trembling with fear, Oliver opened his eyes. He was hurtling through the sky. His heart leaped in his mouth. And then he looked up . . . at a mass of handsome brown, white, and black close-set feathers.

He was being held in the talons of a giant hawk.

He looked down and saw Lizard shaking his fist with empty fury. The hawk swooped and fell through the air, faster even than the supway, leaving the frightened pigeons far behind.

And then, high in the clouds above U Nork, the great hawk turned its head down at him, and in a deep, snarling voice boomed:

"You praised my son! You fed him and saved him from the hunters! He is being raised in the Other Place. He came here on a visit and told me about you. He sent your sock through the steps across the water. He shared your sock, and I knew your smell. No hawk would ever help a human! But you helped my boy, and for that, I will give you one ride—no more than that. But one ride home!"

It was Pale Male's mother! Oliver remembered that time when he had praised Pale Male and left the dead mouse for him on the bed of his little sock.

"Thank you!" was all Oliver could think to say. And then, realizing that he had better choose a destination, added, "Please take me to where those pigeons are going with the little dog!" he said.

For the first time since he had come to U Nork, Oliver almost breathed easy. He looked down at the city, through cloud and snow, as it hurtled past below.

Safe inside City Hall a few minutes later, Blue and Oliver stared at the tiny pellet of ice and the drawing that Rose had sent with it.

Tiny Spot looked up at them intelligently, licking diamond dust from General Boghen's hand. Spot seemed to know that he had completed his mission and earned his meal.

Oliver stared at the drawing. "No, I don't think so . . . It's—" He looked harder and thought for a moment.

"Is it a code? Hieroglyphs of some kind?" asked General Boghen.

Suddenly Oliver had it, clear as day. "It's another rebus! Rose sent us a rebus! Smart girl!" He paused, full of admiration for how clever his little sister was. "It's a blue mark, then fire, and an eye. Blue—Fire—Eye! Don't you see? That's what she's telling us to do. Smart *girl!*"

Blue gulped. He understood now, and he realized that in the end it all depended on him.

"Can you and the sub-chefs do it, though, Blue?" Oliver asked. "Rose must think you can."

"I *think* so. I mean, I was boasting a bit when I said I could shoot a steak to the moon . . . but yeah, I think so." His voice became a strangled mutter. "I mean, I guess I'd better or . . . U Nork is lost. We lose the whole city. Gone for good."

General Boghen seemed almost inspired by Rose's strange idea. "Good lad!" he said, gently mussing his hair. "Gentlemen: to the cannons!"

A few moments later, on the snowy, shaking street, Blue Boghen commanded his little squad of sauce shooters. Lightning flashed in the sky above and the bright advertisements sputtered and sparked and, bit by bit, went out, Blue Boghen gave orders.

"We have only one chance. We have to load it with all the air we can—that means everyone pumping as hard as they can, in shifts, for fifteen minutes at least."

"But, Blue—won't that cause it to explode?" one of the chefs asked.

"We have to take that chance. . . . We only have one shot. I just hope Rose can put the Ice Queen into the line of fire. She'll have to do it perfectly. It's as much on her as it is on us."

"Trust Rose!" It was Oliver speaking. "Trust her. She's quite a kid." And he stared up at the sky, and waited for his younger sister to save the city.

"What have you done, you horrible girl? What did you drop there?"

Ultima, like all suspicious people, was very watchful. And though she couldn't be sure, she thought she had seen Rose drop something into the ever-widening crack in the snow globe.

"What have you done? You evil girl!" Ultima demanded again, grabbing the hammer.

Rose knew she had to distract the woman until the moment came.

"I didn't do anything," she said. "I only—"

Ultima turned toward Rose's classmates, who were standing, silent and zombielike, in one corner of the room.

"Go away," she ordered them. "Now! Leave! I have to deal with your friend!"

The other girls meekly shuffled toward the door and out of the room. Rose's heart rose into her throat at the thought of what Ultima was planning to do.

Ultima watched as the other girls left the room. Her eyes were icy. The door clicked shut.

Ultima came around the desk for her. Rose drew back in fear.

But the look in Ultima's eyes was tender—almost as though she were weeping. She reached out a hand to touch Rose's face. Rose shrank back in distaste.

"My love!" Ultima cried.

Love? Rose didn't know what to think.

Ultima drew close.

"Don't you know why I wouldn't make you my slave? I could not bear it if you lost your will! I want you alive and aware, so that you can live with me. Live with me not because you have to—like your frozen friends—but because you *want* to. Because we need each other."

And suddenly Rose recalled Louis's words: "You have diamond dust in your veins, too."

Before she could speak, Ultima continued. "Don't you see, Rose? You're my . . . daughter. I lost you long ago. They took you far, far away from me, then they brought you to hide you in the snows, the daughter of the Ice Queen. But I have found you now, my one true love! I'm your mother."

"My mother!" Rose said.

"Your mother! You were not made for this small and insignificant life that fate has imprisoned you in. When I came to New York, I came in search of you. That was why I claimed this role—of all the roles that I could have claimed! A fashion magazine! Bah—it was because I needed to be near you. Even to be near your so-called father. Your *father*! That little man! A bad joke—almost as bad as *my* father, the fool—"

Her father? Rose wondered. She expected Ultima to insult Rose's father, but wasn't Ultima's father the famous Flying Visitor? Before Rose could contemplate the news, Ultima was hovering just above her face. She could smell Ultima's heavy perfume as though it were permeating her every pore.

"Listen to me: You are not small, sweet Rose, everyone's baby sister. You are the real Rose, my Rose—strong and powerful, racing through the cosmos, proud and strong, like her mother. Rose! The Snow Princess. Swooping through the stars beneath my celestial wing, mother and daughter—the great Princess of the Northern Snows. Stay with me, my love, and you can have anything you want. Do you want to be the ruler of that tiny city? It's yours. I won't harm it if you only promise to be my daughter again here. Or if you want to stay here and become the ruler of this sad place?" She gestured out of the window at New York. "We can!" Then her voice became low and urging. "I am your true family, Rose, which you have always sought. I am your mother. I am your true family, and we must be together."

Rose was dazzled. As she looked into Ultima's eyes she could see everything that Ultima had promised: a brave, free, powerful Rose doing as she liked and going as she pleased right through the galaxy, protected by a mother who wasn't a worrier but the most famous woman in the world. She wouldn't be cute little Rose anymore, who everyone kissed and no one respected. She would be strong, powerful Rose. . . . She could help everyone, of course, and be kind and everything, and *also*, for once in her life, have the power to do good without having to ask and be "nice" all the time.

And then her eye caught the snow globe, and she thought of Oliver, who had given up his freedom to help her save this tiny city, even when he didn't know it was tiny, because she had asked him to. And who kissed her absent-mindedly no matter how he was feeling. And Rose thought of her mother and father worrying about her. And she thought about her father's bad jokes and good nighttime stories, and her mother's kind touch and gentle voice, and she knew her own mind.

"No!" Rose said. "You're not my mother. I mean, maybe you are—but I don't care. I'd rather stay here with my real mother, who loves me, and my brother, who risked his life for me, and my father, who tells me stories and calls me 'Partly,' than join you and become all cosmic."

"But they are not your family! And this is not your home!"

But suddenly Rose was feeling very sure of herself.

"Your family are the people who love you," she said slowly. "And the people who know a little about your mind, even if they don't know anything about your past. And your home is all the places in the world where you're welcome. They care about me in U Nork. And you were going to ruin it. *But I won't let you!*"

She shouted these last words, and Ultima's face changed terribly as she did.

"You horrible girl," Ultima snarled. "Watch me destroy the city—and claim my diamond!" She raced to the desk and swung her hammer. But Rose held her away, as Ultima stabbed and thrust and the little girl and the Ice Queen began to struggle above the little snow globe on the desk.

The people of U Nork watched as Rose and Ultima fought in the sky above their city. They had heard the argument, of course, but only as distant thunder and low rumblings in the sky above their heads.

"The Ice Queen and the Snow Princess!" they cried now.

Of course, the people of the city did not know that they lived within a tiny snow globe that had sat for years on a dusty shelf in an antique store, and was now shaking on a desk in the office of a fashion magazine in a skyscraper in Manhattan.

Rose was tussling to get Ultima in the right direction without letting Ultima know that she was being pushed into the right place.

Back and forth, this way and that, clutch and hold, pull and push.

The commotion must have been easy to hear in the room next door, since the knob turned again, and Eloise, Wendy, and Stormy were staring inside.

"Do you need help?" one of them asked at last.

"Yes! Obviously!" Ultima cried—and then the cold girls were upon Rose, pulling her from Ultima and throwing her to the floor.

Ultima threw her a scornful and hate-filled look, then went to the desk and greedily peered into the snow globe.

Lying on the floor, supporting herself on one hand, Rose prayed silently that the U Norkers had understood her instructions.

* * *

"One shot, gentleman! One shot!" General Boghen said, walking up and down the lines of sauce cannons. He bristled with pride in his crisp uniform.

"I've got this, Dad."

Blue drew his crew—five or six grave-eyed boys with the same kind of white skullcap that Blue wore—close around him. They listened soberly as he spoke: "Okay. We're going to load the cannon with mustard sauce, since it's the lightest sauce we have, and should travel the farthest. We have one chance to shoot a stream of sauce higher and farther than we ever have, and we have to strike it right through the little crack in the sky." Blue stared up, a little despondently, at the tiny spiderweb crack in the sky. "If we aim right and try hard, I think we can."

"What are we trying to do?" one of the other assistant chefs said. His voice was shaking with anxiety. "Blind her or something?"

Oliver came over and squatted beside him. He put one hand on the chef's back to calm him a little.

"Sort of," he said smiling, and he held open his palm to show the tiny sliver of Ultima's poisoned diamond dust that Rose had attached to Spot's collar. "The sauce is just the force. That's your bullet."

They stared in silent wonder at the tiny shard of ice.

276

Silently and efficiently, as the lightning crackled overhead and the snow fell, the crew of cannoneers went to work. They pumped the cannon full of compressed air, working until their arms ached.

It was then that Blue Boghen saw Ultima's face appear, vast and greedy, above the city.

"Fire!" he shouted. "Fire in her eye! Now!"

At once the sous-chefs set off the cannon—and a stream of sauce, with its little glittering shard at the top, flew through the night air over U Nork, a tiny focused laser of liquid, shooting up against the night sky.

The whole city gasped as the Ice Queen stared directly into the stream.

The liquid flew higher.

Ultima stared down into the snow globe. She pressed closer. What was that sound? Cheering? Cheering coming from the doomed people of U Nork?

And then the door opened. It was Joe Murphy.

"Rose," he cried, "I came to rescue you!" He rushed for the desk.

But the noise made Ultima turn her head ever so slightly away from the globe.

And the stream of liquid struck her on the far left side of her forehead.

$* \quad * \quad *$

On the streets of U Nork, far below, the cheering stopped. There was a gasp of disappointment, and then a slow wail of despair. And then to their horror, Ultima's enormous face again filled the sky. They had had one chance. And they had missed.

For a moment, Ultima looked with rage at Rose. The sauce had struck her forehead. *Splat!* Right by her left temple, above her eye. It would have been funny had it not been so serious. She looked ridiculous, which of course made her angrier.

Suddenly, Rose saw the tiny pellet slipping down her forehead toward her left eye.

Rose held her breath. If Ultima felt it, if she wiped her face at all, it was over.

She had to do something so that Ultima wouldn't notice.

Slowly Rose said, "I lose, Mother. You win. The diamond is yours."

And Ultima laughed and bent over the globe.

Rose watched, still holding her breath.

For a moment, it was as if Rose was watching Ultima Thule in extreme close-up and super-slow motion—as though she could see every pore on the upper left side of Ultima's face: her eye, and the place between her nose and eye, and her forehead. She watched the tiny ice chip slide down Ultima's forehead toward her eye in aching, torturous increments. Would it slide into her eye—or slide by? Oh, no, it was slipping, painful mini-millimeter by millimeter, right by . . .

Ultima threw her head back in triumph. The little pellet of ice skipped on her skin, took one tiny leap, and for a second was lost from sight.

And at that moment Rose realized all she had lost when her plan had failed, and she thought of all the people she might never see again, now gone forever in the fall of U Nork: blustery Louis, brave Blue, the well-meaning SPASM, and above all, her own courageous and kindhearted brother . . . now she would never see Oliver again!

Rose began to let out a quiet wail of grief—

As she did, she saw the tiny sparkling glint of the diamond chip once more—and saw it skip and land right in the corner of Ultima's eye!

For a moment Ultima seemed unaware of what had happened. She looked uncomfortable. She turned to Rose, a look of deep puzzlement on her face. And for a second, mother and daughter, Queen and Princess, Ultima Thule and Rose of Eighty-eighth Street, locked eyes.

"What—?" Ultima began to say, almost gently, and her hand reached for her eye.

Rose swallowed hard. "You're mine, now! You do what I say!"

And Ultima, her mother, looked back at her obediently. Rose didn't know what to say next.

"You just . . . be nice," she said at last.

"Be nice," Ultima repeated dully.

The cold girls looked, awestruck, as Rose gave orders to their mistress. Then they turned on her too, and repeated, in unison:

"We must . . . *be nice!*"

"Yes." Rose felt bolder. "Be nice. From now on, you will stop doing all that, uh, mean stuff." Rose hoped that hadn't sounded lame, but it was the best she could think of in the moment. Then she went to the snow globe and peered into it.

"It's okay!" she said. "Just hold tight. You'll be all right."

Down in the city, the people of U Nork stood in wonder.

"It's okay, everybody," Rose said, her face filling the sky. "Is Oliver there? Is Spot okay?"

There was a long pause. Then she heard a tiny voice that, though it was just barely audible, she knew was Oliver's: "Nice work, Rosie. What are you doing up there so giant-size?" It was followed by an even tinier, but chirpy, bark.

* * *

Ultima sat down with a thud on her desk chair.

Mr. Murphy, whose desperate entrance had almost ruined Rose's plan, said, sheepishly: "Hey, Rose, you'd better get U Nork back to a safe place. Away from here . . ."

"Mr. Murphy," Rose said. She couldn't wait. The questions were rushing out of her. "How do you know about U Nork?"

"Oh. Well. I was kind of there when the city was, as you might say, conceived and constructed."

"You! You mean you're—"

"The one they call the Flying Visitor? 'Fraid so, Rosie. I more or less got this cosmic disturbance started. See, I flew off to Nork when I was just a young man. They had these zeppelins moored in New Jersey, and so, and well, I got in one to write a story about it for the old *World* newspaper, and hit the wrong button and, well, off she went. It was experimental—all enclosed and airtight and so on—and I became the experiment!

"Landed at last in Nork, and I showed 'em pictures of my hometown, just to keep 'em amused. Well, the rest I guess you know. They decided to build their own bigger city—they had gravity just light as air, Rose, you could watch 'em put up a hundred stories the way a child builds a sand castle, just that easy, and then—well, then I married. Fell in love with a Norkian girl. Beautiful, beautiful woman she was, and well—" He looked sadly over at Ultima. "It's a heavy thing, having children gone wrong—even one child among four.

"So my other daughters—queens they became!—hid you away, safe and sleeping, until the time came to wake you up—and now here you are, back again!"

Rose was so stunned by all this news that it took her a moment to penetrate its real core.

"Then, Joe—then you're my grandfather! I'm really and wholly—yours!" It made her feel partly happy, and partly weird.

"Guess so, Rosie. Guess I am, at that." And Joe almost giggled, a sound Rose had never heard from him before.

"But really, you know, Rose, all this family hoo-hah— it's all a little overdone. Sure, you're my granddaughter, Rose, and glad to call you so. But you're those good people's child, too, the ones who love you so. And in another way, you're the daughter of U Nork.

"The way I see it—the way I see it, Rose, a family is just the people you can sometimes share thoughts with, whose minds you know, a little, and whose tastes ya can sort of anticipate—its all those partlys that make a family, not some 'wholly' anything you can put your finger right on. In the long run, it doesn't matter where you come from. All that matters is where you're headed. And you and I are headed home. I'll hold your hand, and we'll take the steps, make one last call in the great square of that huge and tiny city. . . ."

"Sounds good," Rose said, reaching for his hand. "Let's go—Granddad?" It came out as a question rather than a statement.

"Call me Joe, Rose," he answered simply. "It always puzzles me, Rose, this thing about people wanting to know who their ancestors are. Why are people so interested in their ancestors when they already know their relatives? Some of your real ancestors were kinda nice, and some kinda rotten, as you've seen. But you and I—we ask the same kinds of questions, and laugh at the same jokes, and we worry about each other when we have difficulties. We always have. *That's* what makes us family. The rest is all just gossip, even if it takes place in the stars." He looked down at the desk, where U Nork stood still, safe under its diamond shell. "Or deep inside a snow globe, for that matter."

Rose nodded as he spoke. Then she realized that they would have to get the snow globe—the entire city!—back to a safer place, and mend its sky, before she could visit it again. So Rose found some packing tape, and carefully placed it over the crack in the snow globe that held the city. Then, huddling the temporarily mended snow globe under her arm, surrounded by the three friends she had now set free, they cautiously and carefully began to walk back to Medusa Books. Across Forty-second Street and through Grand Central, up Lexington Avenue. Rose bent her head down to the snow globe, the little world in her hands. Even on the busy New York street she could faintly hear the people of U Nork cheering for her, louder and louder, again and again.

A SMALL PARADE AT TWILIGHT

(Rose tells me that thirteen chapters would be an unlucky number, so this is Chapter Twelve and a Half.)

Square Times Square Squared was thronged with people when Rose and Joe Murphy got there. It was the following morning, and by the time they arrived the town had already had a big parade down A5 with the crowds cheering and crying, "Rose! Rose!"

U Nork didn't look any different; the towers were just as high, the streets just as broad, the traffic just as crazy. But now, it felt different to be there. When they arrived at last at Square Times Square Squared, Rose knew it wasn't the biggest square in the biggest city. It was a tiny square inside a snow globe, inside a bookstore off Lexington Avenue.

They had carried her up to the podium set high above the Squared Square, where she found herself surrounded by old-fashioned round microphones, with the names of the U Nork radio stations (URTB, ULUVME) printed on their collars. First, the SPASM gave her a special prize—a numbered ticket to replace the one she had taken on the street that first time she had visited U Nork. This ticket had a simple digit on it: I.

"Rose," the SPASM said, "from now on, that's your number! If there's a line in U Nork—you don't wait in it." Then everyone cheered, and Rose knew that they wanted her to speak.

Rose glanced up at the sky and thought, Most of the people I know are up there, in the bookstore, and I'm really tiny! The thought almost made her dizzy. Then, looking down at the throng of thousands of people, she thought, They don't *look* tiny. They don't know they're tiny. So I can't treat them as if they're tiny. I have to talk to them as if they're big as anything in the biggest town, and still know they're not.

She felt so dizzy trying to keep the two ideas clear in her own head that the only way to keep her mental balance was to start talking. Her shyness, and her fear of mixing up words was still bothering her, but she leaned into the microphones.

"Good people. Friends. U Norkians . . ." Her voice vibrated and echoed around the square and seemed to bounce off the now clear blue Norkian sky.

"We've won a big victory." They cheered. "That was thanks to the bravery and clear thinking of Blue and the general, my brother Oliver, and Spot, and, well, all of you! So, congratulations and nice work." There was a pause.

There was something terribly important that Rose wanted to say next. But she didn't know quite how to put it in a convincing way. So she hemmed, and exhaled as the crowd buzzed beneath her, until at last she let it all rush out. "You see, there's something they haven't told you—the SPASM and the mayor and everyone because they thought you'd be scared. But, well, here it is." And Rose tried, as best she could, to explain what she knew, while the SPASM waved his arms wildly, trying to cut her off. Louis, though, just looked at her with a small, approving smile.

Rose held on to the microphone as she attempted to explain the truth about their city and its history to the people of U Nork, who slowly grew silent as she spoke.

"It looks like you're living in this giant city and everything," she said. "But really, you're just very tiny inside a fragile little glass globe."

The crowd of Norkians fell dead silent. Where a moment before they had been cheering for their beloved Rose, now the entire city was quiet with disbelief.

"It's true!" Rose insisted into the microphones. "The SPASM will tell you. And Louis, too. What I'm telling you is true." And as she looked at their shocked and frightened faces, she realized that just telling them wasn't enough, not unless she could sort of *inspire* them, too.

"It's true," she said again, more softly into the microphone. "It's true, but it doesn't matter that it's true. You've defeated your ancient and cosmic enemy, and you did it through your own actions, and it didn't matter what size you were. Big is big and small is small, but in my opinion, you're really only as big as the last brave thing you've done. And all of you just did a really big brave thing."

Well, that was what Rose had meant to say. But she was still nervous and speaking quickly, so it came out reversed. "A really big thrave bing," is what all the people of U Nork heard her say.

Rose realized what she had said, and blushed in embarrassment. Oh, no . . .

But the crowd, believing in Rose, and taking a moment to think it over, seemed to decide that they liked this new way of saying it, and they began to cry, "A Really Thrave Bing!" "A Thrave Bing with Rose!" And then once again they cheered, louder than ever: "Rose! Rose and U Nork!"

Rose had never felt so relieved and happy in her life. And so for the first time, as she looked out on the field of puzzled, patient faces, she felt inspired. She held out a hand to quiet them.

"But now this hiding thing has to stop. The only way to live," she said, as confidently as she could, "is out in the open, defying your enemies. You can have your life or you can live your fears. And I would rather have my life and face my enemies than hide from them."

"But the Ice Queen is finished, so it doesn't matter anymore whether we hide or we don't," cried the SPASM, who was also on the platform. He really was, Rose thought, in a SPASM. "She's your slave!"

"I don't *want* her as my slave," Rose said, turning toward him. "And she's not the last greedy person who wants your diamond you'll ever meet in the cosmos, big as it is, or the last person you'll be tempted to hide from. Or to hide away . . . Like Sin-Trail Park, where you sweep away the problems you'd rather not see. A park should be a park, not a prison.

"You've seen that you can defend yourselves, if you trust brave people like the Boghens. Trust me: it's like Mr. Murphy—I mean, my grandfather—I mean, the Flying Visitor." Rose wasn't exactly sure how to refer to him, even as he beamed silently at her from the other side of the platform. "It's like that gentleman always says: it doesn't matter where you come from—all that matters is where you're going. And it doesn't matter what size you really are—you were big enough to defeat the Ice Queen, and that's big enough for anyone."

There was a silence from the square. And then the people began to shout:

"Make the Boghens kings! Make the Boghens kings!"

"NO!" Rose practically shouted into her microphone. "No! That's not what I mean at all. Don't make anybody king. Just use your common sense and good judgment and just remember that things are always just as big as your thoughts about them, and I'm sure you'll be fine."

Then, because she couldn't think of what else to say, she said what her mother always said to her at night. "Just . . . trust me," she said. "Just trust me."

There was a long silence. And then the people of U Nork began to cheer. "Use Your Common Sense!" they shouted, and then "Trust Rose!" and "Rose Is Never Wrong!" and someone even began to shout "Be As Big As You Think You Are!"

"Oh, well . . ." Rose stepped away from the microphones. She felt frustrated. She didn't want them cheering her. And she didn't want them reciting slogans. Not even slogans she had supplied. She wanted them to act sensibly.

"Louis . . ." She shrugged. "What can I do?"

"Don't worry about it, kiddo," Louis said. "You done good. You can't help it if people trust you."

"Oh, dear," the SPASM said. "Now they know the truth. And they don't know who they are, or what size they are. . . . They'll be so confused. . . ."

But General Boghen, bristling with new medals—which he had awarded himself—on his uniform, turned to Rose kindly.

"You've told them the truth, Rose. You *are* just as big as the size of the last brave thing you did. And, Rose," he said—looking out across Square Times Square Squared, where the throng was still crying "Trust Rose!" and "Do Like Rose Says!" and "Rose Is Never Wrong!"—"you just did a very brave thing. You told an uncomfortable truth to an unwilling crowd. There's nothing braver."

And so Rose walked down from the podium, holding Mr. Murphy's hand. As she did, she heard the SPASM begin to talk excitedly, and all the people cheer, and the great anthem of U Nork—"What a Burg We Got Here!"—begin to play.

When Rose came down from the podium, she found Mr. Murphy and Blue Boghen, who was holding Spot in his palm. Little Spot leaped up to her, and Rose kissed his ears and held him gently.

"Hey, Rose!" Blue said. He seemed sort of embarrassed by all the attention they both were getting. "Nice rebus."

Mr. Murphy took off his hat, put it on Rose's head, and gave her a big, fat hug.

"Mr. Murphy, what's going to happen to Ultima?"

"Oh, I think she'll be okay. For the moment she depends on your will, and you can keep telling her to be nice. Eventually, you'll have to set her free, and tell her to be nice on her own. She can stay in New York. There are a lot of people like her there. Or go back to the stars, if she wants. She may actually get to be a pleasant daughter over time. Take care of me in my old age and so on."

Rose turned to Blue.

"Blue, won't you come back to New York?"

"No. I have to stay here. Especially if we're ever going to, you know, go back to the universe outside. But I wish we had gotten to know each other better."

Then Rose did something impulsive, but she was sure was the right thing to do.

"Here, Blue," she said. "Keep Spot with you, here in U Nork. He's a hero here, and if I take him home I'd have to watch him every moment, he's so small. Plus, he lives on diamond dust, and I may not be able to get back here for a while. Maybe a long while. And I trust you. You'll keep him safe."

She stroked Spot's small head, and bent down and gave him one last kiss.

"Good dog!" she murmured. "You were the best dog. But you'll be better off here with Blue, where little dogs like you belong. And because you did such a brave thing, I know they'll always care for you, and feed you, and let you sleep on a velvet cushion." And so she wouldn't cry, she pushed him into Blue's pocket.

"Thanks, Rose," Blue said. He had always wanted a dog, too.

And so it was that, at seven o'clock one night, not long after, a procession could be seen making its way across the city of New York toward Central Park, through the now ever chillier autumn air. It was like a small parade at twilight. Leading it was Joe Murphy, slowly waving the flag of the free republic of Greenwich Village that he had taken from the Washington Square Arch. (The publishing company had paid his bail, Rose had learned, and fixed things with the cops.)

Just behind came Rose's now-devoted friends, grateful to her for freeing them from being slaves of the Ice Queen, and also thinking that Rose was pretty cool. They'd all dressed in matching black skirts for the occasion. Bringing up the rear of the procession were the three Cone sisters, grim-faced and purposeful, carrying a strange device that looked a little like a toy catapult slingshot. And in the middle of them all was Rose, very carefully carrying a satin pillow. And on the pillow was U Nork in its snow globe. And beside her, standing watchful guard and making sure that nothing happened to upset the little world, was her proud and grateful brother, who occasionally bent down to kiss her head, because he couldn't help it.

At last they made their way through the Children's Gate, and into Central Park, where the streetlamps had just come on, creating little pools of light. And then they came to the Great Lawn and formed a semicircle around the steps across the water, as they emerged for one last time.

"Wait till the night sky appears!" the eldest of the three sisters declared.

So all of them waited silently as Central Park grew cold, until at last the first stars of the fall evening appeared high above the city and its skyscrapers, and the electric signs came on along the skyline.

For one moment Rose held the snow globe with beautiful U Nork inside it up, high up, all the way out at the length of her arm, so that, to her eye, the two skylines were almost exactly the same size.

"Look," she whispered to Oliver. "Now they're equal."

And then the three sisters solemnly took it from

her, and put the snow globe inside the sling.

"What is that thing?" Rose whispered to Joe Murphy.

"It's the sling of the stars," Joe said. "Watch what happens next!"

As the stars began to glimmer in the sky, the three sisters pulled the snow globe back, way, *way* back, farther and farther, and then, just as the stars began to appear in the darkening sky above the Empire State Building, they let it snap!

Rose gasped at the sight. Surely the snow globe would shatter as it hit a building at the edge of the park.

"It's okay, Rose," Oliver said. "The velocity is constant, so they won't even know it's happening." Rose wasn't quite sure what he meant, but it sounded reassuring.

The globe climbed higher and higher, glittering bright against the violet blue sky, like the released birthday balloon that Rose had noticed the first time she saw the steps across the water, only so much faster, until at last the globe passed higher than the buildings, higher even than the airplanes that flew overhead, beyond their jet contrails, and into the night sky itself.

"It's a star again!" Rose whispered to herself. "I mean, a planet—I mean, a city. I mean, well, it's back in the cosmos." And she watched it travel back to the stars as long as her eyes would let her.

Tears came to her eyes—good tears, tears of wonder. Then she felt a gentle hand wipe them away.

"I know, Miss Rose," Joe Murphy's voice murmured. "Ah *know*. Losing things is hard. And now my daughters will have to close the bookstore, too, as they go back to the stars." He said this very heavily.

"But you said that if the bookstore closed, the city would be over . . ."

"I did! And I was right! The city is all over, but the city we lost was U Nork, which is back where it belongs." He sighed. "Sometimes small is large; sometimes large is very small. As long as there's one person to take a walk down a street, or read a funny book, or listen to what people say— why, then that's all the world you need. Your room is as big as the world, just as the biggest city in the universe can sometimes fit inside a snow globe."

"It depends on your point of view, I guess," Rose said.

"And on what you might call your frame of reference, Miss Rose," Joe added. "You saw U Nork as the biggest city in the world because it was, with the other people in it. That wasn't the way you saw it—that's the way it was. There's always a bigger or smaller frame of reference around. Who knows, Rose? Maybe *we're* just a tiny city in someone else's snow globe." He looked up at the stars. "That seems just as likely as anything else. And maybe somewhere up there in

U Nork there's another snow globe in another bookstore with another city inside it! What's big? What's small? Like you told 'em, Rose: everything is as big as the size of your thoughts about it."

Rose knew that U Nork was now safe, or as safe as cities can hope to be, somewhere in the sky. Taking her grandfather's hand, she walked happily home.

Later that year, for her birthday, Rose's parents got her a parakeet—a beautiful azure bird that chirped and swung on her swing and ate millet from her fingers—because her mother was still allergic to dogs. The parakeet was very bright, and of course she named it Blue.

And every night until the winter came, and it was too cold, Rose would repeat Joe Murphy's words when she and Oliver would take Blue out into Central Park and scan the sky for the city of U Nork, now back where it belonged. "Everything is as big as you think it is," she would whisper to her bird.

It's out there, you know. I think that if you look carefully at night you may see it, a small shimmer in the night sky. And if you listen carefully you may hear the beatings of giant pigeon wings, and even the barking of a brave and tiny dog. That's what Rose thinks, anyway, and Rose is never wrong.